HAPLESS
HERO
HENRIE

HOUSE OF HEROES

HAPLESS HERO HENRIE

Petra James

Illustrations by A. Yi

Kane Miller
A DIVISION OF EDC PUBLISHING

First American Edition 2021
Kane Miller, A Division of EDC Publishing

Text © 2019 Petra James
Illustrations © 2019 A. Yi
Published by arrangement with Walker Books Limited, London.
First published in 2019 by Walker Books Australia Pty Ltd.

For information contact:
Kane Miller, A Division of EDC Publishing
5402 S. 122nd E. Ave, Tulsa, OK 74146
www.kanemiller.com
www.myubam.com

Library of Congress Control Number: 2021930462

Printed and bound in the United States of America
1 2 3 4 5 6 7 8 9 10

ISBN: 978-1-68464-354-7

To Maddy, Frannie and Oskar —
brave hearts three.

And for Kath, who gave us joy.

Hero: 1. A person, typically a male, who is admired for their courage, outstanding achievement, or noble qualities.

Hapless hero: none of the above.

Chapter One

I, Henrie

I KNOW I have to tell you right away.

It was the spark that caused the flame that caused the house to burn.

It blazed a hole in my life.

Besides, I hate not knowing things. I bet you hate not knowing things too.

Not knowing things can be dangerous to your health. It's true.

See this wide-open mouth?

Note to you

I call it "shock jaw."

It happens when you don't know things.

And then you do.

Imagine if a bee buzzed into your wide-open mouth and stung you on the tonsils.

Imagine if your tonsils blew up like a balloon and blocked your throat.

Imagine if you couldn't breathe.

Note to you
Dangerous, huh?

Shock jaw happens a lot when people hear my name first and meet me second. They are surprised, shocked, staggered, startled and stumped to discover I am **Henrie the Girl**. Yes, a girl, girl as in: *I am not a boy.*

Were you expecting that?

◯ Yes　　◯ No

P.S. Only big fibbers answer **Yes**.

Are you a big fibber?

◯ Yes　　◯ No

P.S. If you answered Yes then this is the story for you. There are tons of big fibbers in it. Most of them are related to me.

I bet you thought a story called *Hapless Hero Henrie* would be about a boy because Henrie is a boy's name. And, it is. Usually. But there's nothing usual about my story. Believe me.

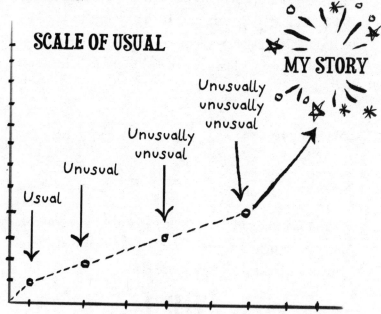

SCALE OF USUAL

MY STORY

Unusually unusually unusual

Unusually unusual

Unusual

Usual

If your full name was Henrietta Madeline Melchior I bet you'd shorten it to something people could say without sounding like their mouths were stuffed full of words, wouldn't you?

What were my parents (not) thinking?

(Not) thinking parents

* Max Marmaduke Melchior, the Third
* Persephone Mathilde Melchior, the One and Only

There's a story behind what they were (not) thinking. I'll get to that soon. But, first, back to your shock.

I think it's really excellent to have a shock on the first page of a story. It's like a stinky sock in the face. It *whacks* you awake.

Are you awake?

○ Yes   ○ No

You can tell already I'm not a hero because heroes don't say much. They talk with actions that make loud sounds and take up lots of space like:

POW!

Crunch! Thwack! BAM! BIFF!

BIC!

But not me. I talk every second of every minute. I've just got so much to say. Especially now. After everything.

I don't even have to draw breath when I talk anymore because I've been practicing how to increase airflow by breathing through alternate nostrils. It's like having two noses.

Pun alert

Two noses are better than one.
Everyone nose that.

Ellie says she doesn't know how so many words can squeeze inside one small person. (It's true. I *am* small for my age. I think my growth spurt might have gone to the wrong house. Alex Fischer who lives four doors down has had at least two growth spurts in the last three months. One of them must have been mine.)

Anyway, who would want to be a hero? You have to wear bad clothes, itchy masks and stay awake all through the night in case a building bursts into flames, a cat gets stuck in the tallest tree in the park, or Mrs. Mellifluey from No. 17 locks herself outside in her slippers and dressing gown. Again.

So, even though I was born into a House of Heroes, this is NOT a story about a hero.

It's a story about what happened after I was born and what has just happened.

It's like there were all these dots around me waiting to be connected and then, suddenly, when I was eleven years, eight months, and nine-and-a half days old, they were.

Henrie Before

Henrie After

12

Sometimes it's hard to know where to begin your own story. Should I begin:

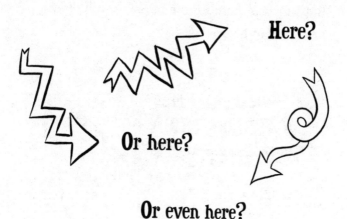

Here?

Or here?

Or even here?

So I'm going to start at the moment everyone still talks about. My birth.

I've heard this story so many times it's just like I was there – having an out-of-body experience. Although, technically speaking, I wasn't really out-of-body because I *was* actually there, but I was only a few seconds old so I didn't have much to say yet. I was gurgling and dribbling and keeping my eyes squeezed shut to block out the bright lights prying into my new eyeballs. (They were 100-watt bulbs at least.)

To tell you the truth, it was all a bit of a *shock* for me. I'd been all warm and cozy, curled up tight and sucking my thumb (yum) and, suddenly, there were stark lights and a room bursting with *shrieks*.

But why was there a room bursting with *shrieks*?

I'm about to get to that.

Chapter Two

Not a Boy

THE THING IS, you aren't the only person who thought I was going to be a boy.

In fact, you have joined a very long line of people who said I was going to be a boy.

Here are three of them:

1) **Dr. Beetle from Mercy Mary Hospital.** He said: "I can deduce by the shape of the bump and my indisputable, indeterminable, inexhaustible, medical experience that this child will be a boy."

2) **Grandfather Octavia Melchior.** He said: "Tradition. That's what makes the House of Melchior great. Of course, this child will be a boy. All firstborn Melchiors are boys."

3) **A crystal gazer called Claire Voyant.** She had stared into my mother's eyes at a fair on the village green and

yanked a hair from my mother's head. Then, she tied it around my mother's wedding ring and held it above her bulging baby bump.

Soon, it began to swing from side to side, like a hypnotist's watch. Claire Voyant closed her eyes and breathed deeply through her inner chakra. She said: "Yes, I can feel the energy pulsing through me, swelling like the restless sea. This child will be a boy."

"Are you absolutely sure?" said my mother, peering into the crystal ball to see the restless sea.

"Of course I'm absolutely sure," said Claire Voyant, covering the crystal ball with her galaxy scarf. The future was for *her* eyes only. "In my forty years of predicting babies, I have never been wrong. My success rate is one hundred percent."

Note to Claire Voyant

Time to make that 99.99 percent, I think.

It was a gloomy winter morning at Mercy Mary Hospital the day I arrived in the world. (I'm not going to tell you the date because you've already got a lot to concentrate on and things are about to get dramatic.)

The corridors were dimly lit and the nurses were slumped at their night stations, counting the hours till they could close their eyes and snuggle into sleep. Snores and snuffles were erupting from the patients' rooms (especially from Mrs. Molly Swift in Room 212. She was snoring up a storm).

The light on the exit sign above the fire escape flickered on and off. On and off. Ticking the night away.

Inside Room 307 of the delivery ward, my mother was gripping my father's hand. This was the moment they had been planning for nine months. It was the beginning of everything.

My father looked at the clock on the wall. **2:58 a.m.** In just 120 seconds, he would meet his firstborn baby boy. Melchior baby boys, you see, were always born at **3:00 a.m.** on the dot. I know this is scientifically impossible, but it's true: Melchior mothers had the most uncannily precise biological clocks. It wasn't because of an ancient prophecy or anything. It was just the way it was and always had been.

My father stared at the second hand as it clicked purposefully around the clock's face. Maybe he was thinking about *his* father, twenty-eight years earlier, welcoming him into the House of Heroes. Now he was about to greet his own son and the heroic future that lay before them.

That's when things started to go wrong.

At **2:59 a.m. and 11 seconds**, I arrived.

I was **49 seconds** early.

Forty-nine seconds might not seem very important to you.

49 not-very-important seconds

1 2 3 4 5 6 7 8 9 10 11 12 13 14 15 16 17 18 19

20 21 22 23 24 25 26 27 28 29 30 31 32 33 34

35 36 37 38 39 40 41 42 43 44 45 46 47 48 49

Forty-nine seconds is just the "blink of an eye" (although, technically speaking, Cyclops is the only one who can "blink with an eye").

Most times, a "blink of an eye" means nothing. But, sometimes, one of them means everything. This was one of those means-everything blinks.

"Here's your beautiful baby – **girl?**" shrieked Dr. Beetle.

(Shriek No. 1)

Of course, he was all ready to say "beautiful baby boy" and see how that rolls off the tongue? It's on account of all those bouncy, bubbly baby "b"s.

"Girl?" screeched my father.

(Shriek No. 2)

"Girl?" screamed my mother.

(Shriek No. 3)

My squeezed-shut eyes startled open at all the noise. Couldn't a baby get any peace and quiet around here?

"That can't be our baby," said my father, pointing accusingly at newborn me. "Where's our baby boy?"

"I don't understand," said Dr. Beetle. "I was so very–"

"Wrong," shouted my father. His face was pale and he put his head in his hands. "This is disastrous," he cried.

Grown-ups think they are good at saying the right thing at the right time but, often, they're not. Disastrous is not a good word to utter at the birth of a baby. **Delightful, delicious, delectable, dainty, darling** are much better words to toss into the air to settle on a baby. Even I could tell that and I'd just been born.

As the Doom of Disastrous settled around me, a nurse tried to give me to my mother, but my mother was sobbing into her pillow. Big, heaving, snotty sobs.

19

"Poor baby," she kept saying. "My poor, poor baby."

Okay, I'm going to stop right there.

I know what you're thinking.

You're thinking:

This is not a great beginning.

In fact, this is the worst beginning of all beginnings.

I hope things get better soon.

It's so sad.

Poor little baby. Blighted at birth.

And you are absolutely right to have all these thoughts (I think you might be a very intelligent reader. I haven't had many of those lately).

This was the only birth I'd been to so I didn't really know what to expect from those who were expecting me.

When I was older, I heard there are often tears and screams at births but they are usually tears and screams of … joy.

Which brings me to two very important observations:

Important observation 1

Q: Have you ever noticed what rhymes with **joy?**

A: _____

Yes, I knew you'd know: **boy.**

Important observation 2

Q: Have you ever noticed what rhymes with **girl?**

A: _____

Yes, I knew you'd know again!

Tons of *hurly burly* words like:

whirl twirl swirl curl

That was me all right: a curly girl.

My parents must have thought so too.

Because that was the last time I saw them.

Chapter Three
A Dereliction of Duty

WHAT A WAY to end a chapter.

Did those words catapult your heart into space?

I'm so proud of that ending I almost want to stop my story there. But I'll keep going in case you're still reading.

You're probably wondering how I know all this stuff about what happened when I was born. I didn't make it up. Honest (although I do have an excellent imagination and a tendency to be dramatic).

You see, there was someone else in the delivery room when all this was happening. Someone who was in the middle of all the shrieks but wasn't shrieking. Someone who's been pretty important to me ever since: Ellie, my mother's little sister. My aunt.

As my mother's and father's and Dr. Beetle's shrieks grew louder and louder, Ellie stepped in with a flourish.

"Hand me that baby," she said.

She knew what was coming next. She knew she had to get me out of there as fast as she could. Once all the shrieking had stopped, decisions would be made. Decisions that couldn't be unmade.

Ellie wrapped me in a blanket like a falafel and, clutching me as tightly as she could, fled down the fire escape – her footsteps **clatter-clat-clattering** on the stairs.

We've been on the run ever since.

Note to you

Ellie doesn't like me saying we're "on the run."
(She's the one who says I've got a tendency for the
dramatic.) "It's more like we're lying low, Henrie,"
she says. "We're just keeping to ourselves at the
moment."

"The moment" has turned out to be eleven years, but
I guess some moments can last longer than others.

Longer-lasting moments

* Going to the dentist
* The night before Christmas
* Sunday night spinach soufflé

My mum and dad had planned to call me Henry
Matthew Melchior so Ellie just tweaked my name for
the birth certificate.

But you're probably wondering about my mum and
dad. What happened to them?

Well, according to Ellie, they were hauled off to
Hero Headquarters, the family business in Moldavia, for
dereliction of duty.

"What duty did they derelict?" I said.

Ellie looked sad. "They didn't have a boy," she said.
"They had you. It was the first time in two hundred

years that the firstborn child of a Melchior wasn't a boy."

"Oh," I said. "So that means I'm historically important?" I was keen to be historically important. Like Queen Elizabeth the First. She's my hero.

"Well, I guess," said Ellie. "But historically important in a dark kind of way."

"What does that mean?" I said.

"Well," said Ellie, "like when King Henry the Eighth beheaded Anne Boleyn."

"Oh," I said. *That* dark kind of historically important. "Are they coming back?"

Ellie looked sadder. "I don't know, Henrie," she said. "It's complicated. I'll explain it all when you're older."

"Oh," I said. "How old?"

Ellie never did answer that question, or any of my other **923** questions, and that was three years ago. I'm nearly twelve now but Ellie keeps saying I'm still not old enough. She must have some terrible things to tell me.

I googled House of Melchior to try to find out some answers for myself, but "No Searches Found" came up, the first time, the second time *and* the third time. (Ellie said she wasn't surprised there was nothing online because the Melchiors were secret squirrels, lived in the Dark Ages and probably hadn't even heard of the World Wide Web.)

I found my dad's business card on page twenty-seven

of a book called *Surviving Impossible Families*.

House of Melchior

Fortes fortuna iuvat

Heroes for the every day since 1818
MAX MELCHIOR: CEO

Solutions to your problems, big and small.

Anonymity ★ Ingenuity ★ Discretion

By appointment only.

I held the card over the gas stove to see if the heat revealed any invisible messages (top tip from *101 Tricks of the Private Eye*), but it burst into flames and set off the fire alarm. Any invisible message was invisible cinders now.

So that's pretty much me:

* historically important – in a beheading kind of way
* a dereliction of duty
* an orphan with parents

When I was little, I was much more hopeful. Whenever the doorbell rang, I always imagined it would be my mum and dad. They'd been searching for me for years and years and were really dusty from looking under beds and in cobwebby attics all over the world, but they were still beyond thrilled to see me.

I'd run into their arms and they'd wrap me in huge hugs and swing me into the air as if I were as light as a cumulus cloud in a spring sky. They'd smell like hot chocolate and raisin toast, and our smiles would be as wide as the sun.

I'm a lot more realistic about the world now. Happy endings like that only happen in dog movies on rainy days.

And it's not that I'm not happy. I love Ellie and Ellie loves me. It's just, sometimes, I feel something's missing.

I don't mean body bits and pieces. I've got all of those.

Body bits and pieces checklist

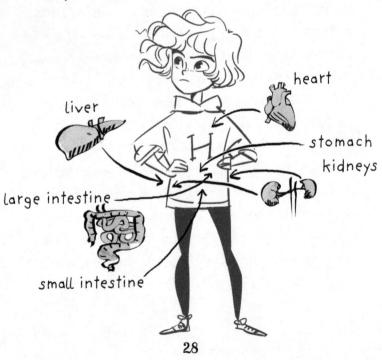

liver

heart

stomach
kidneys

large intestine

small intestine

It's more the stuff in between the body bits and pieces – the stuff you can't put your finger on but you know it's just as important as your heart or your small intestine. Like the sound of my mum's special voice – the one I know she'd have just for me – no one else in the whole wide world.

It's funny how you can miss what you've never ever had, but you can. The ache is the same.

I found Moldavia on a map last year and stuck a pin in it. I'm saving up for a private jet to fly there one day because even though I'm a dereliction of duty I still think I should travel in style. I've only got seventeen million dollars to go (jets are much more expensive than I thought they'd be).

Most of the time I try not to think of my mum and dad, although they still pop into my head when I least expect them.

Last week, I was watching clouds wander through the winter sky and wondered if my mum and dad ever looked at the clouds in Moldavia and thought of me?

Ellie said of course they loved me when I was born and they love me now. I've seen pictures of me as a baby and I was pretty adorable. Maybe Ellie whisked me away too quickly and my mum and dad didn't get a chance to see how adorable I was?

Once upon a time, I used to get really mad at myself. Why wasn't I a boy? If I'd been a boy, my mum and dad would still be here. But if I'd been a boy, I wouldn't be me and I wouldn't have this story to tell you.

Funny how some thoughts spin you in a dizzy little circle and you end up exactly where you started. Stories can do that too. We might look like one big picture of a person from the outside but inside we're a kaleidoscope, made up of hundreds of thousands of good and bad and smelly moments, colliding at all angles.

So, you can see my story had a few pointy angles already. But it took a 360-degree turn in a new direction when the postcard arrived.

Chapter Four

The Saturday of Saturdays

IT WAS A Saturday in the school holidays. All my friends were away and I was bored.

Ellie was at her Mandarin class at the community college and I was home alone, curled up on the chaise lounge, reading *How to be Famous* by U.R.A. Mazeball.

Ms. Mazeball said famous people always thought outside the box. But I was obviously stuck *in* the box because I'd been thinking for two hours and twenty-eight seconds and still hadn't come up with a truly original idea for how to gain fame.

Me

Truly
Original
Idea

FAME!

I checked my twenty-two minute and three second video on YouTube of an ant carrying a bread crumb. It only had ten views (and seven of those were mine).

Outside, I heard the postman whistling, getting off his bike and propping it against the iron railing. Then, I heard his steps on our front porch and the mail slot in the door opening and closing.

I've thought (at least thirteen times) that it would be very helpful if Momentous Moments were signposted. At least then you'd know you had to take an extra-big breath for the shock about to sideswipe your brain. I had no warning at all that the red envelope sitting in the middle of the black-cat-with-the-curly-tail welcome mat was about to change my life forever. But I did notice immediately there were two strange things about it.

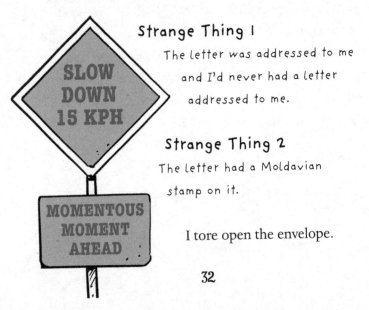

Strange Thing 1

The letter was addressed to me and I'd never had a letter addressed to me.

Strange Thing 2

The letter had a Moldavian stamp on it.

I tore open the envelope.

32

There was a postcard inside and this is what it said:

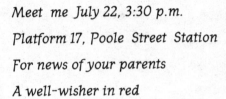

Meet me July 22, 3:30 p.m.

Platform 17, Poole Street Station

For news of your parents

A well-wisher in red

A well-wisher in red. With news of my parents.

This was the most exciting postcard I'd ever seen. But what did it mean?

As the words became loud and louder in my head, I had a tight feeling inside. As if bubblegum guerrillas were blowing up my stomach.

I looked at the envelope. It had been posted two weeks ago. Snail mail.

I looked at my watch. It was 2:45 p.m. on July 22.

I'd promised Ellie, hand on heart, I'd never go anywhere by myself except in an emergency.

emergency: n. (pl. –cies) 1. An unforeseen occurrence; a sudden and urgent occasion for action.

Was this an emergency?

It was certainly an intriguing turn of events.

Should I go? Or should I stay? I could run there and run back. I might even be home before Ellie. But what if I wasn't?

What if Ellie panicked when she walked into a house without me and called the police? Like last time when my kidsitter Edwina stopped to buy us all ice cream and we were twelve and a half minutes late home.

The police arrived with flashing lights and sirens at the same time we did. The tall policeman with frowning eyes told Ellie in a gruff voice that she was wasting taxpayers' money. Ellie said she was a taxpayer too and you couldn't be too cautious in today's world. Then we went inside and ate our raspberry ripple ice cream before it melted.

That was five years ago, and I was practically a

teenager now. Teenagers in books went off by themselves all the time so they could be daring and smart and brave. Some of them even saved the world before breakfast.

I planned to be the best teenager I could so I needed to practice as much as possible. Ellie would understand that, wouldn't she? She'd been a teenager in the old days.

But even as these brave thoughts tore through my head – excited and yelling to each other – I was wondering if I should get a second opinion. I looked out the window for inspiration (Ms. Mazeball said blue-sky thinking was tops), and that's when I saw Alex Fischer.

He was trying out his new skateboard on the sidewalk. His jeans were faded and ripped, and his long floppy hair dangled in his eyes. He was hunched over his skateboard and his kneepads kept slipping down his skinny knees and bunching around his skinny ankles. His skateboard was spotted with blood from his skinny shins.

I opened the front door and stared at him.

He got off his skateboard and stared at me. When he stood up straight, he was nearly as tall as the STOP sign on the corner.

"You're too tall," I said.

Whoops.

I did it again – said the first thing that came into my head. Ellie calls it a "blurt." She said we've all got afflictions to bear, and speaking first and thinking later is mine.

She said maybe I should wait for the second thing to come into my head and say that instead. But the second thing that came into my head was usually wishing I hadn't said the first thing so, technically speaking, I'd have to wait for the third thing but by then I already had another ten or thirty thoughts jumping around in my head and none of them had taken a number like the queue at the delicatessen in Abercrombie Street so how could I tell which thought was which?

Note to you

The average head has about **70,000** thoughts in one day. If you opened my head right now, these are the thoughts you'd see:

* No, you can't.

* That stinks.

* I'm hungry.

* Mr. Sniffles is the funniest cat.
* Say that again and I'll scream.
* Why doesn't time go faster?
* Why doesn't time go slower?
* My big toe's toey.

"I've had two growth spurts in the last three months,"
said Alex Fischer.

"I know," I said.

"And you can't say that," said Alex Fischer.

"Say what?" I said.

"That I'm too tall," said Alex Fischer.

"Well, I just did," I said.

"Well, it's not right," he said.

"Why not?" I said.

"Because it's discrimination against tall people,"
he said.

I looked at Alex Fischer looking (down) at me. I
could see right up his nostrils. There was a piece of snot
huddling in the corner of the left one. It looked like it
had been hiding there for days.

"Well, then," I said, thinking on my feet, "I've got
nothing in common with tall people."

"Can you ride a skateboard?" said Alex Fischer.

"No," I said.

"Me neither," said Alex Fischer. "That's something we've got in common."

I nodded. He had a point.

"Why do you think that anyway?" he said.

"Think what anyway?" I said.

"That you've got nothing in common with tall people?" he said.

"Well, that's obvious," I said. "I see things that are close to the ground and you see things that are close to the trees. We see totally different worlds."

"So?" said Alex Fischer. "That means I see the top and you see the bottom. We've got the whole world covered."

I looked at Alex Fischer. "The whole world covered." I liked the sound of that.

Then I snapped into action and looked at my watch. It was 3:01 p.m. and I really needed someone to come to the train station with me. One lonely eleven-year-old would attract too much attention. Two talking kids would pass in a glance.

Anyway, I could always give Alex Fischer the slip if he cramped my style. Small people can duck and dive very quickly through busy spaces. Tall people tend to linger longer, gazing at the clouds above the crowds.

"How old are you?" I said.

"I'll be twelve in two months," he said.

"Okay," I said. "You'll do." And I filled him in as fast as I could:

Me. Birth. Boy. Not.

Parents. Absent. Aunt. Present.

Note. Mystery. Meeting. Now.

"Let's go," he said, tucking the skateboard under his arm.

I smiled at Alex Fischer. He didn't say much, but that was okay.

I had enough words for both of us.

Chapter Five

An Indecisive Noun of a Man

POOLE STREET STATION was swirling with sound and movement. Shouts, whistles, trains, loudspeaker announcements, the **bumpety-bump** of suitcases rattling and rolling along the platforms.

I'd never seen so many people in one place before. My heart sank. "This is a veritable needle in a haystack," I said. "We'll never find him."

"Or her," said Alex Fischer.

My heart sank even further. "Double the trouble," I said, jumping out of the way as a man with a suitcase barreled into me. People often bumped into me and then looked surprised. I was like a puddle they stepped in first and saw second.

It was all right for Alex Fischer. Tall people were so lofty. Everyone saw them first and stepped around them second.

"We need to look for someone looking for someone," said Alex Fischer.

"We're at a train station," I said. "Everyone's looking for someone."

"This will be different."

"How do you know?" I said. He was sounding enigmatic. "Have you had a mystery meeting at a train station before?"

Note to you
Enigmatic is a fancy word for "mysterious."
See how many times you can say it today.

"No," he said. "But I read a lot. Train stations are always used for secret assignations." He closed his eyes.

"You're not going to see much with your eyes closed," I said.

"I'm activating my inner eye."

"Huh?" I said.

"It's like a waking meditation," said Alex Fischer. "It helps me see things. Just try to clear your head. And remember: a needle in a haystack is sharp."

"Very helpful, not," I muttered.

I closed one eye, and then the other. I could see … nothing.

IT WAS REALLY DARK INSIDE MY HEAD.

"Focus," said Alex Fischer in my ear. Or maybe it was in my head? His whispered words seemed extra close.

"Imagine a door," he said.

I imagined a door. I decided to paint it red. Red is my favorite color.

"Imagine an open door."

I imagined an open door. It was painted red.

"Now, imagine all your thoughts racing out the open door."

I imagined all my thoughts racing out the open door, which was red, and tripping over each over in their haste to be gone from my head.

Wow. I'm thoughtless, I thought, but then I quickly pushed that thought out the red door too because I was supposed to be getting rid of old thoughts, not having new ones.

As my head became an empty vessel, I opened my eyes. As wide as could be. I couldn't believe it. The scene in front of me had transformed. Sounds and shapes weren't colliding anymore. Now, I could see layered ribbons of movement threading through the hustle-bustle of the station:

people catching trains,

people leaving trains,

people meeting people.

I could hear a rhythm in the sounds, too. The braking *gush* of trains pulling into the station; the *hiss* of opening doors; the *bubble* of words, floating free from sentences; the *crackle-cackle* of the loudspeaker …

Slowly, I could see everyone around me flowing into one ribbon of movement or another. Everyone except one person: a man with a small wicker basket at his feet, standing under the railway clock above the sign for platform No. 17.

He had black hair and tortoiseshell glasses, and was wearing a ruby-red jacket.

He wasn't old but he wasn't young. He wasn't tall but he wasn't short. He wasn't fat but he wasn't thin.

Later, when I tried to describe him to Ellie, I said it was like he was trapped between adjectives.

"He sounds like an indecisive noun of a man to me," she had said.

Note to you

He wasn't.

You'll see.

Platform 17

"There," I said, and pointed. "What about him?"

"Could be," said Alex Fischer. "He's wearing red."

"And he's looking at us," I said. "Come on."

As we walked toward him, the man bowed slightly.

I bowed back.

Note to you

Funny how a yawn makes you yawn, and a bow makes you bow. You should try it.

"My name is Albert Abernathy," he said as we drew level with him.

← Alliteration alert

"I'm Henrie Melchior," I said.

"Indeed you are," he said, and held out his hand.

I took it and then remembered I was supposed to shake it. So I did.

His hand was cold and his grip was limp. Like a fish. (Not that I'd shaken hands with heaps of fish.)

Albert Abernathy held my hand and stared at me for so long I thought he might be counting the freckles on my face. Twice.

Freckles on my face counted twice

Ten and a half

Finally, he let go of my hand.

"And this?" he said, nodding at Alex Fischer.

"This is Alex Fischer," I said. "My friend."

Albert Abernathy looked right through Alex as if he was checking out Alex's intestines.

Interesting intestinal fact for you to digest later
The small intestine is longer than the large intestine.

Alex held out his hand too, but Albert Abernathy had already turned back to me.

"Alex Fischer wasn't your friend yesterday," he said.

"Well, he's my friend today," I said, thinking, *How did he know that?* "I'm not supposed to go out on my own."

Albert Abernathy nodded. "Most sensible," he said. "The world is a dangerous place. For some of us."

Alex and I looked at each other.

Creepy, my look said.

Creepy, his look said.

As we stood in a triangle, Alex, Albert Abernathy and me, we could have been the only people at the train station. It was almost as though Albert Abernathy had drawn a force field around us.

I poked the air next to me to see if I could feel a force field, but it was as airy as ever.

47

"I'm pleased you are punctual," said Albert Abernathy, looking at his watch. "Punctuality is highly underrated. But, thankfully, afternoon tea is not." He smiled. "I believe all rendezvous should begin with tea. Shall we?" He gestured to a bench on the platform.

We sat on the bench and he opened the wicker basket. Then he offered Alex and me a paper plate, a napkin and a sandwich.

I looked at the jam soaking through the bread. "Raspberry," I said. "My favorite."

"I know," said Albert Abernathy, with a twitch of a smile.

"How do you know?" I said.

"I've been watching you, Henrie," he said.

"You mean like a stalker?" I said.

Ellie had told me all about stranger danger when I was three. She said it was especially important for *me* to have a heightened sense of it. She didn't say why. She said some things just *are*.

I gulped. *Ellie.*

I'd left her a note, pinned to the pomegranate in the fruit bowl on the kitchen table, but I knew she was going to be so mad at me.

Suddenly, I wasn't feeling as brave as a teenager anymore. My brave thoughts had left without even saying goodbye.

> Dear Ellie,
> It was an emergency.
> And I'm not alone.
> I'm with the tall boy from No. 52.
> Love, Henrie xoxoxo

I pushed the thought of Ellie out through my red door and closed it. I could hear her pounding on the door but she would have to wait till I was ready to open it.

"No," said Albert Abernathy. "I am not a stalker. I am a well-wisher. As I said in my letter."

"What else do you know about me?" I said.

"I know you like Queen Elizabeth I, and you could have scored higher on your last math assignment. I'm sure you will do better on the next one."

That's what Ellie had said too. Grown-ups could be very predictable.

"But who …" I said, dropping my voice and raising my left eyebrow, "… *are* you?"

Note to you

I'd been practicing my rendition of significant sentences in the mirror for a couple of months now and was quite pleased with my progress.

"Indeed," he said. "Who am I?" He took a bite of his sandwich and chewed slowly.

I looked at Alex and he looked at me.

Is "Who are you?" a difficult question?

◯ Yes   ◯ No

"'Who am I?'" said Albert Abernathy, "is quite possibly the most pondered-upon question in the history of life itself."

It is? I thought.

"Indeed," he continued, "when one considers the dimensions of the question, the answers are potentially infinite. For example, I am an only child. I am an Aquarian. I am left-handed. I am a lover of Beethoven concertos. I am a frequent consumer of anchovies ..."

I sighed. Anchovies were stinky, and this was going to be the longest answer in the history of life itself.

"However," he continued, "for the purpose of your inquiry today: I am employed by the House of Melchior: HoMe."

"House of Melchior: HoMe?" I repeated.

"That is correct," he said. "I am Octavia Melchior's private secretary."

Chapter Six
House of Melchior

I SPLUTTERED ON my raspberry jam sandwich.

Octavia Melchior.

Ellie had only mentioned him once and that was with a shudder.

"My grandfather?" I said, spitting sandwich bits at Albert Abernathy.

"Yes," he said, flicking the bits off his ruby-red jacket. "Your grandfather. Head of the House of Melchior. Heroes for the every day since 1818."

"Oh," I said. "Well, can you prove it? Have you got some ID, or something?"

Note to you

Always ask suspicious strangers for ID.

Albert Abernathy smiled. "But of course," he said. He reached into his pocket and pulled out a card.

House of Melchior

HEROES BEGIN AT HoMe

ALBERT ABERNATHY

PRIVATE SECRETARY

"I know you have many questions, Henrie," said Albert Abernathy, as I turned the card over and over in my hand, my head buzzing. "All Melchiors are, by nature, curious."

I stared at him. There were others like me in the family? People who never had enough answers to their questions?

"But–" I said.

"However," said Albert Abernathy, "I suggest that at this particular moment I talk and you listen."

"But–" I said.

"I know this will not be easy for you, Henrie," he said, "but I'm afraid our time is short."

Albert Abernathy looked behind him. I looked behind him too. Was he expecting someone? A strange expression had crossed his face. He saw me looking at him and smiled.

"My family has always served the Melchiors," he said, leaning back against the bench and stretching out his legs. "My father, my father's father, my father's father's father, my father's father's father's father—"

"A feast of fathers," said Alex.

Albert Abernathy and I both startled. Alex had been so quiet I'd nearly forgotten he was there.

It was funny because I'd been thinking exactly the same "feast of fathers" thing. I loved collective nouns almost as much as I loved alliteration.

Some of my favorite collective nouns

* A shrewdness of apes
* A murmuration of starlings
* A parliament of owls

Alex just got triple-plus points for coming up with an alliterative collective noun. I think he might have hidden depths.

Albert Abernathy frowned. "Alex Fischer," he said, tapping the armrest of the bench with the bony fingers of his right hand. The middle finger had a ring with an **M** on it. **M** for Melchior. Then, he looked into the wicker basket. "Oh, how unfortunate," he said. "I have forgotten milk for our tea."

"That's okay," said Alex. "I don't have milk in my tea."

"But *I* do," said Albert Abernathy, smiling with all his teeth. I noticed he seemed to have more than usual and some of the front ones were very sharp.

Albert Abernathy pointed to the newsstand behind us, sandwiched between the ticket office and Donut Delice. "I believe that establishment sells milk." He handed Alex some money. "Would you be so kind as to purchase a small carton, please?"

Alex looked at the newsstand and then at me. I knew what he was thinking. He was thinking: *I can't leave Henrie with someone we've only just met who may or may not be who or what he says he is. I don't trust him. His teeth are too sharp.*

If I were Alex, I'd be thinking that too. And it was true. Albert Abernathy's teeth were too sharp. But then, I'd thought Alex was too tall, and he was turning out to be pretty okay for a tall person. And *he'd* said I was discriminating against tall people. Well, wasn't he

54

discriminating against people with sharp teeth? I sighed. Discrimination was very complicated.

Albert Abernathy had things to tell me. He was only the second person I'd met who knew something – maybe everything – about my family.

Ellie was the first so she knew stuff too, but she wouldn't tell me. She kept it all locked up inside her and I couldn't even peep through the keyhole. I could fit everything I knew about my family on a post-it note.

Dramatic birth
Missing mum and dad
Non-question-answering aunt

It wasn't fair. I was a Melchior. Didn't I deserve to know about my family? Didn't I *need* to know?

Alex Fischer and Albert Abernathy were staring at each other. It was one of those nonmoving moments again. As if we were trapped in a bubble and time was *pinging* off us, unable to pop in and push us along.

"Henrie will be perfectly safe with me," said Albert Abernathy, breaking the stare-off. "We have much to talk about so we shall continue our pleasant conversation until you return."

"It's okay, Alex," I said. I was absolutely ravenous for all the information I'd never had. What did it all mean? Were my parents nearby? My heart pirouetted. Did they want to meet me? Would they like me?

I looked at the stains on the front of my T-shirt. I'd been wearing it for three days.

Note to you
Every day could be significant.
Dress to impress.

Alex got up from the bench. "Okay," he said to me. "But are you sure?"

I nodded. "I'm sure."

"If I skateboard, I'll be extra quick," said Alex.

"Oh, no need to tire those long limbs of yours," said Albert Abernathy, straightening his ruby-red jacket. "A leisurely saunter will suffice."

Alex scowled at Albert Abernathy and jumped on his skateboard.

We watched him wobble his way along the platform.

Maybe he was getting a little better? He stopped outside the newsstand, turned and waved.

I waved back. Then I reached into the basket for another jam sandwich. I couldn't digest news about my family on an empty stomach.

That's when I spied a small bottle of milk, wrapped in a red-and-white tea towel and tucked into the corner.

"Hey," I said. "You did remember the milk." But Albert Abernathy wasn't sitting next to me anymore. He was standing up, grabbing my arm.

"What're you doing?" I said, pulling away from him.

"Hurry," he said, tugging at me even harder. "We must leave. NOW."

"I don't understand," I said, as his fingers gripped my arm like lobster pincers. "OW. You're hurting me."

"You're in danger," he said, dragging me off the bench.

"Danger," I repeated, swiveling my head. "Where?"

"Do you want to know about your family?" he said, leaning down and staring into my eyes. His breath was chocolate-chippy. He must have eaten a chocolate-chip muffin in the last couple of hours.

"Yes, but–"

"Then do as I say," he said. "Without any questions."

He yanked me hard and I stumbled to my feet.

"STOP," I cried. "We have to wait for Alex."

57

But Albert Abernathy was already pushing, pulling me toward the revolving doors that led outside to the main road. As we inched forward, I looked back over my shoulder.

Alex was zooming along the platform on his skateboard, a carton of milk in his right hand. In slow motion, he pulled back his arm, like a baseball pitcher, and hurled the milk at us.

Most aerial missiles go right over my head so I didn't even need to duck, but Albert Abernathy wasn't as lucky. The carton hit him on the back of the head and sploshed open.

He cried out and dropped my arm as milk streamed down his face, into his eyes. I pushed him as hard as I could and he staggered into the revolving doors. The doors swung shut and he was trapped, snarling with sharp-toothed fury.

Then, something hit me from behind.

I fell to the ground.

Chapter Seven
The Oldest Tricks
in the Book

I **OPENED MY** eyes.

Alex Fischer was kneeling beside me, peering so close his two eyes were one.

"Henrie. Are you okay?" he said. "I'm really sorry."

"I'm sorry too," I said, touching the bump on my head. "I think I might have brain damage."

"Can you see five fingers?" he said, holding up his right hand.

"Anatomically speaking, a finger has three bones but the thumb only has two," I said. "So I can see four fingers and one thumb."

He smiled. "I think you're okay."

"What happened?" I said. "I saw you deck Albert Abernathy but then what?"

"It turns out I can't skateboard and throw milk at the same time," said Alex. "I'll have to practice that."

"Did you knock me over?" I said.

"My skateboard did," he said. "I fell off and it kept going, until it collided with you."

"Dumb skateboard," I said.

"It did come in handy, though," said Alex.

"I guess," I said, sitting up.

"I think Albert Abernathy just tried to kidnap you," said Alex, helping me to my feet.

"WHAT?"

"I know," he said. "I can't believe I fell for his phony old milk story. Distracting the enemy is the oldest trick in the book."

"I can't believe you fell for it either," I said. "What kind of sidekick are you?"

"What about you?" said Alex. "You were busy scoffing his sandwiches. Feeding the enemy into a false sense of stomach security is the second oldest trick in the book."

Note to you

The third oldest trick in the book is making you fall for the first and second oldest tricks in the book.

"I wasn't scoffing," I said.

"You've got jam in the corner of your mouth," he said.

I licked the corner of my mouth. He was right. They were particularly delicious sandwiches. I wished I'd managed to eat more before Albert Abernathy had tried to kidnap me.

"Why did he try to kidnap me?" I said. "He was going to tell me things about my family. I don't understand."

"Me neither," said Alex.

"If we hurry, maybe we can find out," I said, pointing to the ground. There was a trail of milk splots leading away from the revolving doors. "Quick!" I said. "Follow those splots."

Note to you

A splot is a cross between a spot and a splat. This is what a splot looks like in case you ever need to follow one.

We ran out into the street, looking left and right, barging through the black-suited, briefcase-carrying commuters streaming into the station from every direction.

Taxis were lined up in front of us and the milk splots stopped at the curb next to the first one in the rank.

"This way," I yelled.

I could see the heels of Albert Abernathy's shiny black shoes disappearing into the taxi. We jumped into the back of the next one in line.

"Follow that taxi," I said to the driver. I'd been waiting all my life to say those three words. I was a natural. I could be in the movies.

The taxi driver turned and smirked at us. "Yeah, right," he said. "You kids have been watching too much Netflix. I'm not moving till you show me your money."

Money! I gasped. Taxi drivers never asked for money in the movies. "But it's a matter of life and death," I said.

"So's my next paycheck," said the taxi driver. "Sorry, kids. Pay up or get out."

I dug deep into my pockets. Chewing gum, a bandaid and a red button. (I'd been searching everywhere for that. It was from my favorite shirt.)

"It's okay," said Alex, leaning forward. "I've got money."

He took out a wallet full of cash and flashed it in front of the taxi driver.

WOW. I'd never seen so much money stuffed into a wallet. Alex was loaded.

"But how, where–" I said.

"I'll explain later," he said.

I turned to the taxi driver. "Hurry, please. He's getting away."

With screeching tires and a hard turn of the wheel, the taxi driver pulled a sharp right out of the rank, and soon we were in the long line of cars heading south.

"Can you see it?" said Alex.

"There," I said, pointing two cars ahead. "The one with an orange sticker on the back of the window."

We sped along the highway until we passed under a big sign saying:

AIRPORT EXIT 500 m

"The airport," I said. "If he goes in there we'll never find him."

Alex nodded. He was gripping the front of the seat with white knuckles.

Albert Abernathy's taxi took the airport exit but drove straight past the terminals.

We followed it until it reached the outskirts of the airport, where there was a small airfield with about half a dozen hangars. A sign at the entrance said:

DO NOT ENTER.

TRESPASSERS WILL BE

PROSECUTED.

"Must be a private airport," I said to Alex.

We watched Albert Abernathy's taxi drive through the gate and onto the airfield.

"Stop here, please," I said to the taxi driver as Alex and I peered out the passenger window.

Beyond the fence, there was a small jet standing by the largest hangar.

The taxi dropped Albert Abernathy at the base of a flight of stairs leading up to the jet, and he hurried up them, two at a time, without looking back.

"What now?" said Alex, turning to me.

"Simple," I said. "We have to get on board that jet."

I leaned forward. "We'll get out here, thanks," I said to the taxi driver.

"You kids know what you're doing?" he said, as Alex handed over the money.

"We do," I said.

"I don't want to read about you in the papers tomorrow," he said.

"You won't," I said. "I'm a Melchior." I pointed to the plane. "That's my family's jet."

The driver looked at the word **MELCHIOR** emblazoned on the side of the jet, and raised his eyebrows. "If you say so," he said.

We got out of the taxi and, with one last look at us, the driver pulled away, shaking his head.

"Let's go," I said.

Alex and I crouched-ran through the gates.

"This way," I whispered, spying a stack of crates. We huddled behind them, catching our breath and looking around us.

As you know, I've been saving up for a jet so, luckily, I knew a bit about them. "It's a Cessna 680 Citation Sovereign," I said, poking my head above the crates to check out the Melchior jet. "It seats nine passengers and the luggage hold is big enough for us to hide in."

"They've just finished refueling," said Alex as a truck pulled away from the jet.

"Okay. Now," I said.

We sprinted across the tarmac, ducking and diving between planes until we reached the jet. A man was loading supplies into the cargo hold on the other side of the jet, but his phone was ringing and he was walking away from the plane to take the call. This was our chance.

I pointed left and right with my hands to give Alex instructions – like FBI agents on TV when they don't want the bad guys inside to know they're outside – but Alex shrugged his shoulders and mouthed WHAT?

Note to you
He obviously hasn't read Chapter Five, "The Power of Nonverbal Communication," by Ms. Mazeball.

"On the count of three," I whispered, holding up three fingers. "Round the back. Follow me. ASAP."

Note to you

ASAP is Alpha Sierra Alpha Papa in the NATO Phonetic Alphabet. It's like the crack of a whip in times of great drama.

We raced around to the other side of the jet and clambered up the small stepladder leading into the hold. Fear was flooding through my head and I stumbled on one of the steps, making a loud **clank**. We froze as the **clank** tumbled all the way down the steps and splattered at the bottom.

"Okay?" whispered Alex.

I nodded. I couldn't speak. Fear had gobbled up all the air inside me.

We reached the top of the ladder and peered inside the hold. It was gloomy-dark but we found a corner behind two large packing cases and huddled in.

As I crouched into the darkness, I looked over at Alex. He was surprisingly compact for a tall person hiding in a tiny place.

"I'm double-jointed," he said, seeing my stare. "I can fold my limbs up and make myself really small."

Handy, I thought. Maybe Alex was more like me than I'd realized.

I curled up as tight as I could too and, soon, the roar of the jet's engines filled the hold.

We were taking off.

Chapter Eight

The Long and the Short of It

WE RATTLED OUR way into the air, feeling every bump and sudden jump, up and up, through the clouds.

Finally, the plane reached cruising altitude and the engines settled into a deep hum. But my head was still roaring. The last two hours had been the most action-packed of all the hours in my life so far. How could a mystery note, a secret assignation, a raspberry-jam sandwich man and an attempted kidnapping squeeze themselves into 120 minutes?

And now we were flying to who knew where?

If pinches didn't really hurt, I would have pinched myself.

Breathe, I said to myself in a calm voice. Like the one Ellie uses if I've had a bad dream. She always strokes my hair too. If only Ellie were here with me now. (Although it would be triple squashy if she were.)

I could hear Alex snuffling. How could he sleep at a time like this?

I was rearranging my legs for the twentieth time when a flashlight suddenly shone in my face. I blocked the light with my hands, and kicked Alex. He grunted awake.

"Well, well, well," said the voice behind the light. "We meet again. Somehow, I thought we might."

I didn't need to see the face to know the voice. It was Albert Abernathy. We'd been rumbled.

"Unless you are particularly eager to remain in your present state of discomfort," said Albert Abernathy, moving the packing crates so he could see us, "I suggest you join me in the main cabin. I assure you it's far more luxurious there."

I stretched my legs out and stood up slowly. Alex stood too, banging his head on the ceiling as he did.

"Ouch," he said.

"You are tall for a boy," said Albert Abernathy.

Note to you
Told you.

We followed Albert Abernathy through the door of

the hold into the main cabin. It was bright with light and warmth, and deserted, except for us.

Despite at least three-quarters of me being cold and tired and grumpy, the other quarter of me was thrilled to be flying in a jet at last. Albert Abernathy was right. It was far more luxurious here. The seats were wide and inviting, and there was tea and coffee and chocolate cookies too.

"How did you know we were on board?" I said, sinking into one of the leather seats. It crinkled comfortably around me.

"This is a Cessna 680 Citation Sovereign," said Albert Abernathy.

"I know," I said.

"You should also know then that the jet's state-of-the-art, infrared imaging security system registers the slightest imbalance," he said. "An unaccounted-for safety pin would alert our sensors. Two unaccounted-for bodies were, therefore, impossible to miss."

Whoops. I must have skipped the infrared imaging security system chapter.

"So, we've played right into your hands?" I said. Our Great Taxi Chase and Jet Stowaway had landed us back where we'd started. In Albert Abernathy's clutches.

"That is an accurate assessment of your predicament," he said. "But I rarely fail in my endeavors. And besides, I *am* holding the winning hand."

"What winning hand?" said Alex.

"I have information and you want it," said Albert Abernathy, flashing his front teeth. Then he frowned at Alex. "Mr. Fischer," he said. "Somehow you keep materializing where you are least expected. You are proving to be stickier than Velcro."

"He's with me," I said. "Where I go, he goes."

"So it would seem," said Albert Abernathy. "Alex Fischer, however, was not part of my brief." He paused. "But, since our last encounter, Mr. Fischer, I have had time to conduct some inquiries and it appears you will not be missed. At least, not for the time being."

Alex blushed. All the way from his throat to his forehead. I stared at him. Why was he blushing all the way from his throat to his forehead? What did Albert Abernathy mean? What about Alex's family? Surely someone would miss him?

I knew Ellie would be missing me. At least once she'd stopped blowing a gasket and was able to think like a rational person again.

Now that I thought about it, I didn't really know anything about Alex. He'd just appeared a couple of months ago. With his skateboard. Outside my house. I'd never seen anyone else coming or going from his house.

He didn't go to my school. Did he even *go* to school?

Alex was becoming more mysterious by the minute.

Evidence that Alex was becoming more mysterious by the minute

1. He has stacks of money. This is very helpful when we have to pay for things like taxis, but having this much money at our age isn't normal. Ask any nearly twelve-year-old.

2. No one was going to miss him. "At least, not for the time being."

Alex and I had some Very Big Talking to do. But his explanations would have to wait. I was boiling like a kettle with all the other questions bubbling up inside me.

"Are we going to Moldavia?" I asked Albert Abernathy.

"Good heavens, no," he said, helping himself to a cup of tea and a cookie. "A decidedly chilly prospect at this time of the year."

"Aren't Hero Headquarters in Moldavia?" I said. "In a castle?"

"Once upon a time, yes," said Albert Abernathy. "But castles are notoriously expensive to maintain. And terribly drafty. Your grandfather relocated HoMe to an old cotton mill about eleven years ago."

73

"But the letter you sent me had a Moldavian stamp," I said.

"A small but effective ruse," said Albert Abernathy. "We are a clandestine operation, after all. It suits our purpose for competitors to believe we are still in Moldavia." He smiled. "Knowledge is power. And the pursuit of power keeps us all employed."

"Why did Ellie take me from the hospital when I was born?" I said. "She said I was in danger."

Albert Abernathy nodded. "Yes, that is what she believed," he said.

"Why?" I said. "Why did she believe that?"

"That is a very long story, Henrie," said Albert Abernathy.

"Can you make it a very short story?" I said.

"Perhaps." He looked at his watch. "We have some time. What do you know about the House of Melchior?"

"Not even a post-it note amount," I said.

Albert Abernathy dabbed the corner of his mouth with a napkin. "Well," he began, "HoMe was established two hundred years ago by your great-great-great-grandfather, Phineas Percy Melchior. Phineas was a lawyer, a philanthropist and a connoisseur of human behavior, and he realized there was a need for a House of Heroes. Or, to be more precise – boy heroes."

"Why?" I said. "What's so great about boys?"

"At the time, boys roamed the streets in pickpocket gangs. They possessed all the qualities Phineas required: they were small, nimble, quick thinking, fearless. They could slither into spaces and blend into a crowd. They had excellent hearing and could eavesdrop from a great distance. Their senses were finely wrought; their reflexes incomparable; their memory sharp."

"But girls were all that," I said. "And more."

"That may be," said Albert Abernathy. "However, girls in the 1800s were considered far too proper. Their dresses and shoes were entirely inappropriate for speedy getaways through alleys. They did not practice sword fighting or aspire to noble deeds. Needlework and tea parties did not feature in *The Hero's Handbook*. Accordingly, girls were excluded from HoMe and then, as if by some evolutionary validation of this practice, no girls were born to the children of the House of Melchior for two hundred years."

"Until me," I said.

"Until you," said Albert Abernathy, nodding. "Of course, HoMe has had to evolve to a certain degree over the years. The labor and education laws of the late nineteenth century saw to that. However, HoMe's essential character is still very much what it was when Phineas Melchior established it in Victorian England."

"You mean No Girls," I said.

"Precisely," he said.

"But it's the twenty-first century," I said. "Not Victorian England."

"Progress and change have swept through some parts of the world," said Albert Abernathy, "yet other pockets remain unchanged. Tradition is a powerful force, and many people fear change. They fear what they cannot control. They fear the unexpected."

"Even when the unexpected was just me?" I said. "A baby?"

"When that baby was a girl, yes indeed," he said. "Ellie took it upon herself to remove you from the possibility of danger before that danger had the opportunity to arise."

I shivered at his words: *Before that danger had the opportunity to arise.*

"Are my parents at the House of Heroes?" I said. "Do they know I'm coming?"

"The answer to your first question is both yes and no," said Albert Abernathy.

I frowned. What did *that* mean? Did Albert Abernathy ever speak in a straight line?

"Well, are they excited I'm coming?" I said.

"I'm afraid I am unable to comment on their

psychological states," said Albert Abernathy.

"What can you comment on?" I said.

"Unfortunately, very little," he said.

"What about kidnapping?" said Alex.

Albert Abernathy turned to him. "Did I force you to stow away on this jet, Mr. Fischer?" he asked.

"Not exactly," said Alex. "But you tried to kidnap Henrie at the train station. You sent me on a wild-milk chase."

"Oh, that," said Albert Abernathy. "Purely a misunderstanding. No harm done."

"The milk didn't think so," I said.

"If you *were* so convinced of a wrongdoing," said Albert Abernathy, "did you report the incident to the police?"

Alex and I were silent.

"I thought not," said Albert Abernathy. "Indeed, *I* am the one with a bruise on my head. *I* am the one with milk stains on my favorite jacket." He sniffed the green lining of his jacket and his nostrils peaked in distaste. "The sourness lingers still.

"And you have continued to indulge in your criminal spree," he said. "You followed me to a private airport, trespassed on private property and stowed away on this private jet."

"But–" I said, my thoughts racing before my words. Albert Abernathy was twisting the life out of the truth. Squeezing it through a sausage machine till nothing like a sausage remained. Now *we* sounded guilty and *he* sounded innocent. But that wasn't right.

Wasn't the truth the truth? Wasn't it hard, like a diamond or a nugget of gold? Albert Abernathy was a slippery one. He had an answer for everything and, yet, he answered nothing.

"No, you're wrong," I said, sitting up straight. "We haven't stowed away on this private jet. This is the Melchior jet and I am a Melchior."

"Indeed," said Albert Abernathy, nodding. "I can see that you are."

"Please buckle your seat belts and prepare for landing," said the pilot over the intercom. "We'll begin our descent in ten minutes."

"I guarantee your landing will be more comfortable than your takeoff," said Albert Abernathy as he settled into a seat behind us.

Alex and I clipped on our seat belts. I glanced at him but he was staring at the back of the seat in front of him. Maybe he was sleeping with his eyes open?

Note to you
Horses can sleep with their eyes open.
You could practice this at school.

As Albert Abernathy's words about Alex darted about in my head, a chill spread through me and doubts began to leap on top of each other – clambering for a loudspeaker in my brain. I thought Alex was on my side, but maybe he wasn't? My thoughts were running back and forth across speed bumps, shuddering all the way through me.

It was Albert Abernathy's fault. He had made the truth sound so curly. But maybe it was? Maybe everything I thought was true wasn't true at all?

Was there something fishy about Alex Fischer? Did he know stuff about me? He wouldn't be the only one. Everyone seemed to know more about me than me. *Why* would Alex know about me? *How* would he know about me?

I snuck another glance at him. He looked just like he usually did, but maybe he was thinking evil thoughts? People should change color when they are, so the rest of us could **look out – evil about.**

The plane banked to the left and began to dive into a gray cloud. My stomach began to drop too. I looked out the window but the haze of cloud was obscuring the land below. Where were we?

I had so many questions to ask Albert Abernathy. To ask Alex. To ask Ellie. Questions were swarming around me, like a frenzy of bees. I was far away from Ellie, the only family I had ever known, and about to land in the middle of people I had never met. People who might have the same name as me, but people who were strangers all the same. Strangers who might want to harm me.

Ellie had snatched me away from danger eleven years ago. Was I now walking straight back into it? I wanted to be brave. I really did. But maybe it's easier to be brave when your feet are on the ground – not up high in an endless sky.

Ellie would know how I was feeling. I wouldn't even have to tell her. She always knew what color I was on the inside, just by the sound of my voice.

The plane began to descend and as the clouds parted, I realized I couldn't stop whatever was going to happen next. I was about to plunge down a roller coaster with bone-rattling speed and I had to hold on as tightly as I could for as long as I could. I felt sick and excited at the same time.

As the wheels of the plane lowered, I closed my eyes and took a great, deep breath.

I'm about to meet my family.

Chapter Nine

What to Expect When You're Not Expected

HAVE YOU EVER hoped for something every second of every day for as long as you can remember?

I bet you have so you'll know just how I was feeling as the wheels of the plane got lower and lower. Because that's the thing about hope. It's the biggest question mark in the world and all your favorite things are squeezed behind it, like guests at a surprise party, squished and quiet in the dark.

For eleven years, eight months and nine-and-a-half days, I had hoped, really deep down, in a dark place I didn't visit very often, that my mum and dad would come for me and we would live happily ever after.

Note to you
With Ellie, of course. I couldn't live happily ever after without Ellie.

I know eleven years, eight months and nine-and-a-half days is a long time in my life because it's exactly all of my life, but that's hope for you. It just powers on, and sweeps you along with it. Until it doesn't.

I was about to find out for sure if my mum and dad wanted me. And if they didn't want me, well, the question mark would become a period. And nothing came after a period. It was the end. Of everything.

Suddenly, I couldn't breathe. My fingers grasped at my seat belt. It was a giant python, curling around me, suffocating my insides.

"What's wrong?" said Alex. "What are you doing?"

"Breathe ... can't ..." I gasped. "Plane ... stop ..."

"But we haven't landed," said Alex.

"Can't wait," I said, still struggling with my seat belt.

Alex leaned forward. "Take this."

He handed me a sick bag. It was yellow.

Is yellow a good color for a sick bag?

Yes   No

I looked at the sick bag and then at Alex. "I'm panicking," I said. "Not throwing up."

"I know," said Alex. "Put it over your mouth and try to breathe slowly. Breathe so loudly all you can hear is you. Okay?"

I put the bag over my mouth and closed my eyes – concentrating on my breath, rising and falling. In. Out. In. Out.

"What's going on?" said Albert Abernathy, poking his nose through the gap in the seats. "Is everything all right?"

"Yeah," I mumbled. "Just sniffing the sick bag."

"She's fine," said Alex, leaning toward me and blocking Albert Abernathy's view. "Are you?" he whispered to me.

I nodded. Air was flooding back into me – a tidal wave of calm.

"Look," said Alex, pointing out the window. "There's the runway. We're landing."

I watched the ground coming closer and closer. I wanted to land and didn't want to land at the same time.

With a final flurry of noise and a wheel hop, we landed on the tarmac, the plane shaking with braking speed as it fell from sky to earth.

"Please remain seated with your seat belts fastened

until we are outside the tin shed," said the pilot.

Alex turned to me. "Okay?" he said.

"Okay," I said, scrunching up the sick bag.

"We'll get some answers and then we'll go home."

I nodded. I had to trust him. He was the only friend I had right now.

We were silent as the plane taxied to a stop outside a large tin shed.

Albert Abernathy got out of his seat and walked to the front of the plane, even though the seat belt sign was still on.

"Follow me," he said as he passed. Then he stopped and looked back at me. "Your father had panic attacks when he was a boy," he said.

He did? I stood up quickly in case Albert Abernathy was going to keep talking about my dad, but he was opening an overhead bin at the front of the plane. He took out two puffer jackets and handed a green one to me and a black one to Alex.

"You'll need these," he said. "Winter is here."

With a shoulder heave, he pushed the door of the plane and it opened with a sucking-out of air.

A cold wind slapped my cheeks and I pulled the jacket tight around me. The sky was rain-blue and deepening in the twilight.

At the base of the steps leading down from the plane, there was a black limousine with shaded windows. A driver got out of the car and watched as we descended. He was dressed in a uniform with an **M** on his lapel – **M** for "Melchior." With a nod to Albert Abernathy, he opened the back door of the limo.

"Thank you, Andrews," said Albert Abernathy.

"I trust you had a pleasant journey, sir?" said Andrews.

"Most pleasant," said Albert Abernathy. "I assume everything is ready?"

"As instructed, sir," said Andrews, glancing at Alex and me as he spoke.

"Excellent," said Albert Abernathy. He gestured to the back seat and I climbed inside. Alex followed me and bumped his head on the limo door getting in.

"All right, young sir?" said Andrews.

"Fine, thanks," said Alex, rubbing the side of his head.

Albert Abernathy sat opposite us and began to check messages on his phone.

As the limousine sped along quiet roads, I watched the blur of passing countryside. Night had fallen, and sheep and cows were blobs in the dark. My eyes were heavy and I really wanted to close them, but I remembered what Mrs. Petrie had said about "fight or flight" in biology.

She said when you're in an unfamiliar, maybe even dangerous situation, your body gets ready to defend itself, or run like the wind.

This was definitely an unfamiliar, maybe even dangerous situation. I had to be alert.

After driving for about half an hour, we turned off the main road into a narrow driveway, bordered by willowy trees, ghostly in the beam of the headlights.

A few minutes later, we stopped in front of tall wrought-iron gates that had a huge **M** in the middle of them.

A security camera whirred from left to right and the metal gates swung open. The gravel on the driveway crunched beneath the wheels as we drove up and around the road.

"Is this it?" I said to Albert Abernathy as the car swooped to the left and then stopped.

"If by 'it' you mean our destination," he said, looking

up from his phone, "then, yes, this is it."

I breathed in. *This is really it, then. What I've been waiting for all of my life.*

Andrews opened the back door and we all climbed out.

A large brick building, four stories high and shadowy in the moonlight, stood in front of us. It was an old factory, imposing and grand, like a stern relative from the past. Its red bricks had weathered centuries of rain and shine and stories.

To our left, there was a huddle of strange shapes and awkward angles. I could see half an engine and maybe a third of a cotton loom from long ago.

"Our industrial garden," said Albert Abernathy, following my gaze. "Much less maintenance than a real garden and machines rust so beautifully in the outdoors."

I shivered. My gut was telling me it was a bad idea being here, and Ellie told me to trust my gut. (Except when it's hungry. Hungry guts just think about themselves.)

Alex was looking up and down and around as if he couldn't believe where he was and what was happening either. I bet he was having a gut reaction too.

This is your gut speaking.
Do not go into that scary place.

I needed to get him alone so we could talk. ASAP.

We followed Albert Abernathy up the steps to the main door. I knew we were in the right place because there was a sign hanging on an angle at the entrance:

HOUSE OF HEROES
NO GIRLS ALLOWED

"Welcome to HoMe," said Albert Abernathy.

Chapter Ten

Home is Where the Heart is

ALBERT ABERNATHY PULLED back the security door and turned a key in the rusty lock.

The door creaked open and we entered a huge hall with high ceilings and exposed steel beams. Our footsteps echoed on the marble floor as we walked into the heart of HoMe.

A spiral staircase in the middle swept up and around to the next floor. A statue of a man with a top hat leaning on a cane stood next to the stairs.

"Is that one of my ancestors?" I said.

"No, that is Lord Acton, a British politician," said Albert Abernathy. "He was famous for the quote: 'Absolute power corrupts absolutely.' Phineas believed the

Melchiors should always remember this so Lord Acton has become part of the furniture. He goes where we go. This way, please," he said, leading us past Lord Acton and into a corridor with a series of rooms running off it.

"Most of these rooms are for visiting operatives," he said. "The family's rooms are on the second floor. The third and fourth floors are used for conferences and training purposes."

"Where does all the hero stuff happen?" I said, looking around for signs of hero activity. It was deadly quiet.

Maybe the heroes were having afternoon tea?

"Hero coordination and monitoring of assignments takes place in the heart of HoMe," said Albert Abernathy. "The Control Center."

The Control Center! I couldn't wait to see that.

"Are we going there now?" I said.

"I'm afraid not," said Albert Abernathy. "The Control Center is top secret and strictly off-limits to guests. I'm sure you understand the need for security and secrecy."

"But I'm not a guest," I said. "I'm a Melchior."

"That may be," he said. "However, you are completely untrained in hero ways. Melchior boys are schooled from birth in the ways of the hero world."

I scowled. Albert Abernathy didn't have to tell me (or you) I wasn't a hero. I (we) knew that already. The non-hero facts about me were indisputable.

Non-hero fact 1

My hair. It was wavy and bobbed up at awkward angles, like a ship in a storm. Everyone knew that hero hair should be neat and tied back in a ponytail so it could swing from side to side like a pendulum, marking out moments of drama. If only I had hair like Pippi Longstocking. Her plaits swayed right then left when she rode her horse.

Non-hero fact 2

Heroes rode horses. But horses were too far off the ground for me. I could never ride into town on a horse like Pippi Longstocking.

Non-hero fact 3

No parents. Pippi and I both had missing parents, but Pippi lived by herself. I didn't want to live by myself.

At the end of the corridor, Albert Abernathy stopped outside a door and opened it. It was some kind of classroom, with desks and computers. The back wall was covered with a huge map of the world, dotted with red circles, arrows, post-it notes and red pins.

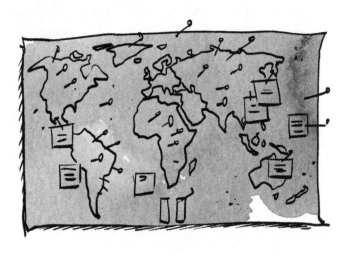

"A map of HoMe's operational bases," said Albert Abernathy.

I looked at it closely. Most countries had one or two pins sticking into them. "What do the pins mean?" I said.

"They show the reach of HoMe," he said. "It is one of the largest privately owned companies in the world, with franchises run by operatives who have passed the HoMe Hero Training Course."

YOU HAVE PASSED THE
HoMe
HERO TRAINING COURSE
YOU HAVE DEMONSTRATED

excellence in Kindness and Courage and have been

accepted into HoMe at one of the following levels:

Level 1: Bronze Operative (BO)

Level 2: Silver Operative (SO)

Level 3: Gold Operative (GO)

Albert Abernathy pointed to a pin. "Each pin denotes a HoMe base, usually peopled by around half a dozen staff. A base is similar to an embassy but is open to anyone seeking help, regardless of national allegiance. All the bases are connected to each other and to the Control Center here, where, among other things, data from every mission undertaken is processed and stored." He smiled. "Information has become quite the currency in today's world."

"How do the levels work?" I said.

Albert Abernathy nodded at me. "You have a curious mind, Henrie," he said. "It's very simple. Each assignment is graded and handed to the appropriate level of operative. Trainee heroes, for example, receive only Level 1 assignments, such as tracking a person's movements to confirm or deny suspicions others may hold about them."

"You mean spying?" I said.

"We prefer to call it Observational Resolution," said Albert Abernathy. "We help people dispel doubts about someone. One way or the other."

I looked at Alex. *SPYING*, I mouthed to him. Alex nodded.

"Operatives progress through the levels until they reach Gold," continued Albert Abernathy. "GOs are called upon for the most delicate and complex of missions: disputed inheritances, lost people, behavioral improprieties and so forth."

He ran his fingers lightly over the map. "I like to think of HoMe as an intricate global cobweb," he said.

I shuddered. Cobwebs had spiders.

At the front of the room was a blackboard with writing on it.

HERO HOMEWORK

Chapter Seven from The Hero's Handbook: Seemingly Impossible Missions (SIMs)

Scenario: The person next to you on the train has a secret note stuffed in his shoe.

Your mission: Retrieve this note.

Task: In 50 words or less, outline how you would achieve this discreetly, without the person's knowledge.

NB: Solutions to SIMs must not involve magic or widespread mayhem. A small degree of mayhem only is acceptable.

Albert Abernathy turned to Alex. "And now, Mr. Fischer, I must ask you to wait in here, please," he said.

"No," I said. "Alex stays with me."

"I'm afraid Mr. Fischer's presence here is unexpected, Henrie," said Albert Abernathy. "You are about to meet your long-lost family. I think Mr. Fischer will understand that both you and your family require some privacy at this time."

"I don't want–" I started to say but Alex interrupted me.

"He's right, Henrie," he said. "You have to do this alone." He looked around the classroom. "I'll be okay here. Come and get me when you've finished."

"Thank you for your understanding, Mr. Fischer," said Albert Abernathy. "I'll organize some refreshments for you."

Alex pulled out a chair and sat down at one of the desks. "I'll do the homework while I'm waiting," he said, picking up a copy of *The Hero's Handbook* that was sitting on top of the desk.

"Well, I'll see you soon, Alex," I said.

"Yeah," he said. "See you soon."

Albert Abernathy closed the door behind us.

"He'll be all right, won't he?" I said. This was my gut speaking again. It was being especially insistent today.

"Why, of course, Henrie," said Albert Abernathy.

"What on earth do you imagine could possibly happen to Mr. Fischer?"

"I don't know," I said. "But strange things are happening today."

Albert Abernathy smiled. "What seems strange today will be less strange tomorrow," he said. He paused and stared at me. I knew he was about to say, "Trust me," but he stopped himself. And I was glad. Everyone knew that people you shouldn't trust always said, "Trust me."

What else people you shouldn't trust always say

* I'm right behind you.
* I'll bring chocolate.

Albert Abernathy and I continued walking and then turned right into a larger corridor. This one was lined with paintings – unsmiling faces in high starched collars with flared nostrils staring down at me.

"Are they all Melchiors?" I said.

"They are indeed," said Albert Abernathy. "This is a portrait gallery of your ancestors."

I peered at the faces. People didn't seem to smile much in the old days.

I read the names as I walked by them.

Phineas Percy Melchior

*Thaddeus
Nathanial
Melchior*

Maximillian George Melchior

Oliver
Thomas
Melchior

Sebastian
John
Melchior

Timothy
Charles
Melchior

Alexander
Frederick
Melchior

"What about that one?" I said, pointing to an empty space.

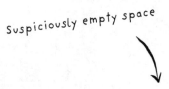

Suspiciously empty space

Albert Abernathy frowned. "Ah, yes," he said. "I'm afraid we don't talk about him."

"Who?" I said.

"Henry Horatio Melchior," said Albert Abernathy. He spoke the words slowly as if they were painful to say.

"Henry?" I said. "Like me."

"In a manner of speaking," said Albert Abernathy.

"But who was he?" I said. "What happened to him? Why isn't his portrait here? Why don't we talk about him?"

"Patience, Henrie," said Albert Abernathy, as we rounded the corner and stopped outside a large oak door. "You'll learn the family history soon enough. But first, the library. You'll be comfortable in here while I'll let Mr. Melchior know you have arrived."

He opened the door and I followed him into the largest library I had ever seen. It was lined with bookshelves that reached nearly to the ceiling. At every corner of the room there was a ladder on wheels so you could whizz from one wall of knowledge to another.

I couldn't wait to show Alex. I knew he read a lot but I bet there were books in here he'd never even heard of.

A boy with thick black hair was sitting at a large table in the middle of the room, hunched over an iPad.

"You're back," he said, his eyes fixed to the screen as he zapped monsters in the video game he was playing. I could see a monster creeping up behind him, ready to munch his head off.

"Indeed, I am, Finn," said Albert Abernathy.

"Who's that?" said the boy called Finn, seeing me and pointing.

"Please don't point, Finn," said Albert Abernathy. "You know it's rude. This is Henrie, Max and Persephone's daughter. Your cousin."

"What? My cousin?" said Finn, with mouth wide open. I watched as the monster munched him. "But … but I don't have any cousins. And she's … she's … a girl."

"Yes, that does seem to be the case," said Albert

Abernathy. "Once again, you have managed to articulate an obvious truth. Henrie *is* a girl and she will be staying in the guest wing."

"Oh no she won't," said another boy, sliding down the ladder in the far right-hand corner.

I hadn't seen him when we came in. He must have been tucked in the dark at the top of the ladder.

"Ah, Carter," said Albert Abernathy. "I was wondering when you'd appear. Eavesdropping again? Well, at least I don't need to repeat myself since you've already heard me relay the pertinent information to your brother."

I stared at my cousins. I was as shocked as they were. Carter and Finn. They were like chalk and cheese. Or spaghetti and roast beef. Carter was tall and spaghetti lean, with blond hair and blue eyes. He stood next to short, brown-eyed, roast-beef Finn.

"We're not having a girl here," said Carter. "You know it's not allowed."

"Your grandfather has invited Henrie to stay," said Albert Abernathy. "You would do well to remember this is his house."

"Not for much longer," muttered Finn. "Gramps is getting more doddery by the day."

"That's enough," said Albert Abernathy, frowning at Finn. "Your grandfather will explain the situation at dinner tonight. Please be punctual."

Explain the situation. Was that me? I wondered.

"But–" said Carter and Finn at the same time.

"I said later," repeated Albert Abernathy, more loudly. "And boys," he said, turning as he walked away, "be nice to Henrie. I'm leaving her in your care while I inform your grandfather she has arrived."

He closed the door.

Finn and Carter stared at me. I stared back. It was my first stare-off with them so I didn't intend to lose.

I was feeling confident because I'd won the annual **STARE-OFF** last year, narrowly beating Will Distemper who said he only blinked because a fly tickled his eyelash.

The seconds marched by and none of us twitched an eye muscle.

But then my eyes started to water. I tried opening them even wider. That helped. For about two seconds. Oh no! I could feel a blink building up.

"Look out," said Carter, suddenly. "Behind you."

I turned. And blinked.

Oldest trick in The Stare-off Book

Making your opponent fall for the
"Look out, behind you" trick.

Oh no! I was falling for the oldest tricks in every book today.

"Ha-ha! Sucked in," laughed Finn.

"Yeah, she won't be any trouble," said Carter, smirking. "Whoever she is."

I could feel tears welling in my eyes. Tears from not blinking, and tears from his words. They didn't want me here. I had wanted a family for so long, but I didn't want *this* family. Not these two anyway.

"Wait till my parents get here," I said.

Carter and Finn exchanged a look.

"She doesn't know," said Finn, smiling, but not in a nice way.

"Doesn't know what?" I said.

Carter smiled in the same way. Now they looked exactly like brothers. Nasty brothers.

"No, she doesn't," he said. "But she'll find out soon enough. Come on, Finny. We've got stuff to do."

"Find out what soon enough?" I shouted, chasing after them. "Wait."

But when I reached the door and looked down the hallway, they had vanished.

Doesn't know Doesn't know Doesn't know
Doesn't know Doesn't know Doesn't know
Doesn't know Doesn't know Doesn't know
Doesn't know Doesn't know Doesn't know
Doesn't know Doesn't know Doesn't know
Doesn't know Doesn't know Doesn't know
Doesn't know Doesn't know Doesn't know
Doesn't know Doesn't know Doesn't know
Doesn't know Doesn't know Doesn't know
Doesn't know Doesn't know Doesn't know
Doesn't know Doesn't know Doesn't know
Doesn't know Doesn't know Doesn't know
Doesn't know Doesn't know Doesn't know
Doesn't know Doesn't know Doesn't know
Doesn't know Doesn't know Doesn't know

"QUIET!"

Doesn't know Doesn't know Doesn't know
Doesn't know Doesn't know Doesn't know
Doesn't know Doesn't know Doesn't know
Doesn't know Doesn't know Doesn't know
Doesn't know Doesn't know Doesn't know
Doesn't know Doesn't know Doesn't know
Doesn't know Doesn't know Doesn't know
Doesn't know Doesn't know Doesn't know
Doesn't know Doesn't know Doesn't know
Doesn't know Doesn't know Doesn't know
Doesn't know Doesn't know Doesn't know
Doesn't know Doesn't know Doesn't know
Doesn't know Doesn't know Doesn't know
Doesn't know Doesn't know Doesn't know
Doesn't know Doesn't know Doesn't know
Doesn't know Doesn't know Doesn't know
Doesn't know Doesn't know Doesn't know
Doesn't know Doesn't know Doesn't know

Chapter Eleven
Family Matters

I SNIFFED BACK my tears and wiped my nose on my sleeve.

Now that I was alone in the library, it seemed like the most enormous room I had ever been in. Bookshelves loomed above me, like skyscrapers blocking the sun.

I could hear a strange noise in the silence, as though the thousands and thousands of words within the pages of all these books were shouting at me, catching my cousins' words and tossing them from book to book, shelf to shelf, aisle to aisle.

"QUIET!" I yelled.

I knew it was silly, yelling into silence, but hearing my own voice made me feel a little better.

I walked along the bookshelves, reading out some of the book titles. "*Atlas of World History, The Historical*

Apothecary Compendium, *The Diaries of Samuel Pepys*, *The Selfish Giant* by Oscar Wilde, *Oliver Twist* by Charles Dickens, *Revelations from the Weird World of Mushrooms …*"

When I got to the **M** aisle, I spied a leather-bound book, propped up on a stand in the center of the shelf. It looked very important.

I walked down the aisle and stopped in front of the book. **THE HOUSE OF MELCHIOR: A HISTORY** was stamped on it in fancy gold letters. The leather was faded brown and had a deep kind of scent – as though it was layered with years of smells.

I opened the book. The first page was a letter. The paper was yellowed and the handwriting was in spidery ink.

Probably written with a feather, I thought.

I looked at the name at the top of the letter. Phineas Melchior – my three-greats grandfather. I began to read.

Phineas Percy Melchior
Solicitor
South Kensington
London
The 23rd day of October in the year 1818

My dear Thaddeus,

The city sleeps, but I do not. My heart is rivaling the loudest drum in the mighty jungles of Africa. And, before you ask, I did not partake of periwinkles for my supper.

It is impossible to marshal my thoughts in an orderly fashion so I shall begin at the beginning. Today, I encountered a pickpocket. You will not be astounded by this revelation. These bands of sewer rats infest our city, scurrying in and out of its labyrinths, intent on thievery and sleight of hand.

I had concluded my business at JW Sneath and was admiring a silk kerchief in the window of Rochford & Sons when I felt the quiver of a movement. One pickpocket too many had found themselves in possession of my belongings so, on this occasion, my response was unnaturally swift.

I grabbed the hand that had attempted to part me from my silver and held fast. The thief struggled as best he could but hunger had weakened his resistance and, ironically, it was he who proved to be the easiest of pickings.

Oh, what a sight beheld me. He was a ragged thing of a boy. Perhaps ten years old, or younger. Sunken cheeks and pitiful eyes. A boy the same age as my own Oliver, who eats three hearty meals a day and dreams of delights in his warm bed each night.

I saw too vividly the future of this boy before me: transportation and hard labor, if he was lucky. The hangman's noose, if he was not. Sorrow coursed through me as I gazed at this wretched creature of God.

As it so happened on this particular day, my mind was also consumed by a difficult case (thinking upon it had obviously sharpened my reflexes): a dispute involving an inheritance due to the widow Blancmange (the most pious of women) and a man claiming to be her long-lost nephew and, therefore, the rightful heir to her sister's fortune. I knew this "gentleman" was a blaggard of ill repute, but of his falseness I had no proof.

And in this manner, two troubling circumstances suddenly collided.

I considered all the reasons boys make excellent pickpockets and, with a blinding realization, surmised that their stealth and speed were exactly what I needed, but for the purpose of good. Consider it a social experiment, if you will (although I am sure you will seize upon other words with which to describe it), but I have decided to grant this boy a second chance. To take him into my house, engage him to spy upon this "gentleman" and deliver to me the irrefutable proof that this scoundrel is an opportunistic fortune seeker.

My dear brother, I value your counsel but I suspect you will believe I have taken absolute leave of my senses.

Your loving brother,

Phineas

Thaddeus Nathanial Melchior
The Manor House
Littlebury
Saffron Walden
Essex
The 25th day of October in the year 1818

My dear Phineas,

Have you taken absolute leave of your senses?

So astonished am I by your letter, I can barely compose a response.

Your words are before me, but they fail to arrange themselves in a comprehensible fashion. This boy, of no family, no morals and no education is, as I write, residing in your house? In dangerous proximity to your five precious sons?

You are more likely to be murdered in your bed than save this unfortunate's soul.

My desire to circumvent your folly has driven me to precipitous action.

I am arriving by the noon train and shall present myself at your door forthwith.

I only pray that I am not too late.

Your most disturbed brother,

Thaddeus

THE EVENING STANDARD

THE 4TH DAY OF NOVEMBER IN THE YEAR 1818

NEFARIOUS NEPHEW

Widow Blancmange of 44 Grange Gardens, Pinner, Middlesex, was present in court to witness the morally deficient fraudster claiming to be her long-lost nephew jailed in Highgate for his most heinous of crimes. The weeping widow thanked her solicitor Phineas Percy Melchior for exposing this rogue and warned all vulnerable widows to beware young men with charming smiles and wily words.

I slammed the book shut as someone coughed.

Albert Abernathy had crept up behind me, very quietly.

"I see you got along well with your cousins?" he said, eyeing the snot on my sleeve with a raised eyebrow and handing me a crisply ironed hankie.

"Have I got any other cousins?" I said, taking the hankie and blowing my nose. "Those ones are horrible."

"Indeed. They are the spoiled sons of a spoiled son," he said. "But I see you've found The Book." He touched it gently. "Not that I'm surprised, of course. Melchiors are drawn to it like magnets. To know your past, Henrie, is to know your future."

"What happened to Phineas and Thaddeus?" I said.

"They went into business together and established HoMe," he said.

"How did HoMe work?" I said.

"At first, boys were hired to pass messages to those between whom messages should not be passed, or possibly monitor a gentleman's movements after dark. As the boys became more skilled, their tasks became more elaborate. They performed great services to many people who had no one else upon whom to call and, eventually, the boys of HoMe became known as heroes.

"When Phineas and Thaddeus retired, they handed the business over to Phineas' six sons."

"Six?" I said. "Didn't he have five?"

"He had five biological sons," said Albert Abernathy. "Phineas adopted Henry, the boy he rescued from a life of crime. He came to love Henry as his own and Henry lived and worked alongside Phineas' sons. But when Phineas died, there was an incident involving a missing bag of gold and three of the sons blamed Henry. The whole business cast a long shadow through the family. The gold was found eventually, but by then Henry had vanished. His guilt or innocence was never fully proven. To this day, he divides the family still."

"Is that why his portrait is missing from the hall?" I said.

"Yes," said Albert Abernathy. "Your uncle, Caspian, removed it. He believes that a rotten bloodline remains rotten to the core."

"Do you believe that?" I said.

Albert Abernathy smiled. "It is not my place to believe or disbelieve," he said. "However, my observation has been that jealousy and deception cross bloodlines with great glee."

"Oh," I said.

"You see, Henrie," said Albert Abernathy, leaning close, "your presence here is a shake-up. For all of us."

"Is that good or bad?" I said.

"That is a question I cannot yet answer," he said.

"But events are now in motion and they shall unfold – one way or the other." He stared into the distance as he spoke and I wondered what he was thinking. "First," he said, interrupting himself, "it is time to meet your grandfather. He is waiting."

Chapter Twelve
Terrible Truths and Shocking Secrets

WE WALKED BACK into the foyer and under the spiral staircase to a small room nestled in the far corner. My grandfather's study.

A fire was blazing in the room, and an old man with wispy white hair was asleep in a leather chair, his glasses perched on his nose and a book in his lap.

As the smoke curled in and around the room, it smelled like a lazy winter morning.

Albert Abernathy put his finger to his lips. "We'll come back later," he said quietly. "Your grandfather hasn't been well."

We turned to leave but a deep voice stopped us.

"I'm just resting my eyes, Albert. I have been

expecting you." The old man was awake and looking at me with murky blue eyes.

"Henrie," he said, holding out his hand. It was covered in motley brown spots and as dry as a summer leaf. "At last," he said. "Come closer, child. I want to look at you."

I moved toward him as he studied me – from top to toe. Then, he smiled. "You're very like my mother," he said. "Your great-grandmother. You have her nose."

"I do?" I said, touching my nose.

"You do," said Octavia Melchior. "I've waited a long time for this day."

"It's nice to meet you," I said, "but I want to go home now."

"You *are* home, child," said the old man, smiling again and patting my hand. "*This* is where you belong."

"Where are my parents?" I said.

"Ah, your parents," he said, the smile leaving his lips. He dropped my hand and turned to Albert Abernathy. "You may leave us now, Albert. I wish to speak to my granddaughter alone."

"As you wish, sir," said Albert Abernathy. A flicker of annoyance crossed his face, but he composed himself quickly. I don't think he liked being left out of conversations.

We watched him open the door and close it softly behind him.

"Albert has been with me for many years now," said Octavia Melchior. "I trust him with my life, but he is not family. And some words should be heard by family alone."

"Are my parents dead?" I said in a half voice. "Is that why they aren't here?"

"Goodness, no, child," he said. "Why do you think that?"

"Everyone looks the other way when I ask about them."

"Your parents aren't dead," said Octavia Melchior. "But they have been missing from my life for many years now."

"Why?" I said. "Where are they?"

"It's a long story," he said. "A story that started nearly twelve years ago."

"When I was born," I said.

"When you were born," he said. "The first girl to be born into the Melchior family for two hundred years."

"Everyone keeps saying that, but I don't understand," I said. "Why was that such a big deal?"

"Of course you don't understand," he said. "How could you comprehend the force of history on the present and the future? We are who we are because of the people who came before us, the people who shaped our spirit, our character. And because of who we had always been, I'm afraid your birth *was* a big deal."

"How?" I said.

He sighed. "I have been imagining this conversation for many years, Henrie. Ordering and reordering the words in my head, trying to make them sound as they sounded to me all those years ago. But memory is an unreliable master," he said. "It plucks an essence but leaves so much behind – the color of the moment, the quick of the emotion. Memory revisits the people we once were. But by then we have left these people behind. And, sometimes, we have buried them deep with pain. Because, sometimes, it is easier to forget."

"Forget what?" I said, my voice trembling. "What do you want to forget?"

I knew it. Something terrible had obviously happened to my mum and my dad. Something Ellie couldn't talk about. Something Octavia Melchior couldn't talk about – even now.

"'The evil that men do lives after them,'" he said, looking into the fire. "Do you know who said that?"

"Um … you?" I said.

Octavia Melchior smiled. "No, it was William Shakespeare," he said. "I think of those words often." He closed his eyes again.

When was he ever going to tell me the truth? I thought.

"A deep truth is difficult to articulate, child," said Octavia Melchior, as though he was reading my mind. "But the truth, as you must hear it, is this."

He paused and I could see him steeling himself.

I steeled myself too. *Is it always better to know the truth?* I wondered. *I guess I'd know once I'd heard it. But by then it would be too late to take it back.* My heart began to pound. *Maybe I should have asked for a sample of the truth?*

Like a patch test to see if you're allergic to something.

Finally, Octavia Melchior spoke. "Max and Persephone left HoMe eleven years, seven months and fourteen days ago," he said. "And I have heard nothing from them since."

"Did they leave to find me?" I said.

"No, I'm afraid they did not leave to find you," he said.

"Why not?" I said. "Is it … is it because … they didn't want me?"

Didn't want me. Didn't want me. Didn't want me. Didn't want me. Didn't want me. Didn't want me. Didn't want me.

"Oh, no, Henrie," he said, his voice breaking. "They wanted you very much."

"Well, where are they then?" I said. "Why haven't they been searching for me?"

"They haven't been searching for you," said Octavia Melchior, "because … because … I told them you were … **dead**."

Chapter Thirteen
The Very Definition of Alive

DEAD.

There's no way around that. It's a lump of a word, dragging everything down with it. Now, it was echoing all around me, in the cackle of the fire and the hiss of the flames. And in the silence swinging between us.

Dead. Dead. Dead. Dead. Dead. Dead. Dead.

Octavia Melchior lowered his head. He had unleashed the DEAD word and now he couldn't even bear to look at me.

Well, I couldn't bear to look at him either. How could he have told Mum and Dad I was dead when I was obviously the very definition of alive? I put my hand on my heart just to reassure myself. It was beating quadruple time now.

Year after year, I had believed my mum and my dad were thinking of me every second of every minute of every hour of every day. Missing me with all their hearts. Imagining my first birthday, my first steps, my first loose tooth, my first bike, my first word …

Note to you

It was "snail."

Because that's what I'd been doing for them. I had eleven notebooks bursting with thoughts for them. Little details they might want to know about all the big and small and in-between moments I'd had in my life so far.

But my mum and dad hadn't been thinking about me. They hadn't been imagining anything at all about me because they didn't know I was a living, breathing me. They thought I was a dead me.

"Why did you tell them I was dead?" I said, when I could finally find my words.

"Why?" repeated Octavia Melchior in the quietest of voices, his head still bowed. "Such a small word for the biggest question of all."

He raised his eyes slowly and looked at me. "Your birth undermined the very future of HoMe," he said. "Max was due to inherit the business and his son after him. But he didn't have a son. He had a daughter. You."

Me.

"Your birth threw generations of the family business into chaos."

Chaos.

"We needed time to think. *I* needed time to think, but things moved beyond me too quickly. Ellie took you from the hospital. We returned to HoMe, and Max and Persephone were inconsolable. They argued, and Persephone blamed HoMe. How could they bring a baby girl here?" He paused. "Angry words shattered many nights."

"But what did it matter?" I said.

"Yes," said Octavia Melchior, smiling sadly. "What did it matter? At the time, I can only say it mattered very much. It was the way we had lived for two centuries. But now …" He paused. "After seeing exactly what it has done to my family, it seems to matter very little.

"One day, Henrie, you will understand that the bonds of family and tradition are unlike anything else," said Octavia Melchior. "They can bind you to strength, and blind you to destruction. After your birth, things began to fall apart. HoMe was already beset by economic concerns as the reality of technological change impacted upon us. Personal, discreet service was at the very heart of HoMe, but technology and social media made information gathering so easy, so impersonal. Our demise seemed inevitable. We had to be stronger than ever. I had to break the unraveling doubt that had begun to erode Max from the inside out."

He took a deep breath and I waited. I had waited eleven years to hear this story. I could wait a little longer.

"Max and Persephone resolved to leave HoMe," he said, "to start a life with you, their new family. But *we* were their family. I couldn't let Max forsake everything that was to be his. To lead HoMe into the future was his birthright. His duty. To make it once again the greatest House of Heroes ever known. I had to do something."

His words were fiery and he didn't sound weak and old anymore. The man who had pushed my parents out of my life was here in front of me.

"So you told them I was dead?" I said, forcing out each word.

"Yes," said Octavia Melchior, his voice retreating once more. "How little I knew of the human heart and its tremendous capacity for pain. Time and grief has made me understand this a little more."

"What happened then?" I said.

"The news of your 'death' didn't make Max and Persephone turn back to HoMe," he said. "It tore them apart completely. It obliterated any hope they had had for a life that included you." He paused and took a deep breath. "And they blamed me."

"But why didn't you just tell them the truth?" I said. "That I was alive? That would have solved everything."

Octavia Melchior grimaced and pain flashed across his face.

"By then," he said, "I was trapped in a web of my own lies. Trapped by my pride. I couldn't tell them the truth. I was already a monster in their eyes. Telling them the truth would have made me even more so.

"Max and Persephone slipped away one summer's night not even a month after your birth. They took nothing with them. Nothing to remind them of HoMe. Nothing to remind them of me."

He rested his head against the back of the chair. A log on the fire fizzed and a flame sparked high.

I was silent. What could I say? No words could fill the enormous holes between us. Holes Octavia Melchior had dug so deep.

"So you see, Henrie," he said. "History repeats itself. Just as my ancestors failed Henry Melchior, I have failed you. I have been the most foolish of men."

Well you got that right, I thought.

"But now, I need to ask you something," he said.

I watched him as he thought carefully about his words.

"Do you think," he said, "maybe one day, not now, of course, but sometime, in the months or years to come, you could try to forgive me? I would wait for as long as that took if I thought there was any hope."

Hope, I thought. I knew about hope. I had been hoping all my life. But my grandfather's hope was smashing my hope into thousands of piercing pieces.

"I … I don't know," I said. "There's an awful lot to forgive."

"Yes," he said, with a sad smile. "There is an awful lot to forgive. And if you feel there is too much, I do not blame you. I am beyond blame now."

I stared at my grandfather's old face, his heavy words playing over and over in my heart. My mum and dad were out there, somewhere. I might never know where they were. They might be dead already. Or they might die never knowing I was alive and looking for them. There were so many "might"s.

Ellie didn't like the word "might." "It's a flimsy excuse of a word," she said once. "Yes, things *might* be this or they *might* be that, but, equally, things might *not* be this or they might *not* be that as well. How will you ever know if you don't try?"

Thinking of Ellie made me remember something else she'd said. I took my grandfather's hand and knelt down in front of him. "I had a big problem once," I said, "and Ellie said when a problem is too large, you should break it down into little pieces. Like cutting up a chunk of steak so you can eat it more easily."

"Sound advice," said Octavia Melchior, nodding and squeezing my hand. "Is that something you think you could do?"

"I could try," I said. "The first thing we have to do is to find my parents and tell them I'm alive. The rest of it can wait."

Octavia sighed and sat back in his chair again. "I have

been searching for them for years, child," he said. "I have hired private detectives around the world. I even hired a Super Sleuth, a man said to be the best at finding people who do not want to be found – Timothy Fischer."

"What?" I said, jumping up. "Did you say Timothy Fischer?"

"Yes, that is his name. I believe he is very famous in sleuthing circles."

"Is that Fischer with a 'c'?" I said.

"I believe it is," he said. He pointed to the bookshelf. "There is an invoice from Mr. Fischer in the fourth book on the third shelf – the blue one – *The Adventures of Peregrine Pickle*."

I ran over to the bookshelf and took *The Adventures of Peregrine Pickle* off the shelf.

"Open it," said Octavia Melchior, watching me.

I opened the book. The pages in the middle had been hollowed out.

"It's hollow," I said, looking up at him.

"There should be something inside the hollow," he said.

I looked down. "A piece of paper."

"That should tell you what you want to know," said my grandfather. "I have kept this search secret from everyone. Except Albert, of course. Increasingly, he has become my eyes and ears."

I unfolded the piece of paper and read it out aloud.

INV 42

Octavia Melchior – HoMe

Part payment for services rendered

Hours of sleuthing: 44.5

Timothy Fischer

Super Sleuth Inc.

"Well?" said Octavia Melchior. "Have you found what you were looking for?"

"Yes," I said. "It's Fischer with a 'c.'"

"And is that important?" said Octavia Melchior.

"It might be," I said, looking at him. "If Timothy Fischer has a son called Alex."

Chapter Fourteen

Deception for Dinner

A DEEP GONG sounded as I was about to ask my grandfather more questions. It bounced off the walls and rang through the hall.

"Ah, dinner," said Octavia Melchior. He looked relieved. His face was gray and his wrinkles were drooping toward his chin.

I knew that confessing stuff was exhausting. That happened to me once when I had to tell Mrs. Gertrude it was me who wrote STINK-A-LOT on the blackboard (only because Sam Huddle had dared me to).

My grandfather rang the bell by his side and Albert Abernathy opened the door a nanosecond later. I bet he'd been eavesdropping. Probably with a glass pressed against the door. That was a very good way to hear a conversation you weren't supposed to.

"Dinner is served," said Albert Abernathy.

"Can you bring me a tray, please, Albert?" said my grandfather. "I'm too tired to see everyone."

"Certainly, sir," said Albert Abernathy. "It's Cook's special tonight. Pheasant kidney cutlets."

"Tea and toast will do for me," said my grandfather. "Tell Caspian I'll speak to him later. When I am in the mood for his questions."

"Follow me, please, Henrie," said Albert Abernathy. "The dining room is this way."

As we left the room, I looked back at my grandfather. He was asleep already. The weight of all those missing years swirling around him.

I felt heavy too. Full of so many things I didn't know if I wanted to know.

"Where's Alex?" I asked Albert Abernathy. "I've got something very important to tell him."

And he has stacks of very important things to tell me, I thought. His father's a Super Sleuth? Searching for my parents? I knew there was something suspicious about Alex Fischer. Suddenly appearing outside my house. Not a responsible adult in sight. Wads of cash. Available on the spot for an adventure.

He had a lot of explaining to do.

I waited for Albert Abernathy to reply but he

kept walking. Maybe he hadn't heard me? He was walking very quickly now.

Alex is probably in the dining room already, I thought as I ran to catch up to Albert Abernathy.

The dining room had a long mahogany table and a crystal chandelier that hovered above it like a jewel thief poised above a glass cabinet.

Six eyes swiveled to stare at me as we entered.

"So, you're Henrie," said a tall man with a small scar across his forehead, standing by the fireplace. "The boys told me you were here."

"Who are you?" I said.

"I'm Caspian, your uncle. Finn and Carter's father. Your father's brother."

"Oh," I said, looking closely at Caspian, wondering if my father looked anything like him. Caspian had dark hair and a thin mouth. He was wearing a three-piece suit with a red tie.

Carter sniggered. "*Oh,*" he mimicked. "She hasn't said anything interesting yet."

"It's a shock," said Caspian. "For all of us." He glanced

at Albert Abernathy and a look passed between them. "Henrie is discovering a family she never knew existed. And we ..." He paused and forced his lips into a smile. "*We* are discovering that someone we thought was dead is miraculously alive."

"Some people should stay dead," muttered Carter.

"Yeah," said Finn.

"That's enough, boys," said Caspian, sharply. "Henrie is your cousin and you will make her feel welcome. It's the least we can do. She has been without us for too many years already. We must try to make amends for the hardships she has suffered."

"I haven't suffered hardships," I said. "I've missed my mum and dad, but I've had Ellie. She's looked after me."

"Ah, yes, Ellie," said Caspian, sneering. "The same Ellie who abducted you from the hospital and kept you hidden for many years. I warned Max about marrying into that family but, of course, he wouldn't listen. Oh, no. Max always knew what was best and now–"

"Don't you dare say anything bad about Ellie," I said.

Caspian smiled. "I see you are loyal, Henrie," he said. "And loyalty is a commendable quality." He moved closer, his eyes looking deep into me. "Loyalty to your family is the most important loyalty of all. And by family I mean, of course, the Melchiors. You will understand that, I hope, once you get to know our history better. Every Melchior child learns the family history as soon as he is born. In this way, it becomes part of who he is, as important to him as the air he breathes."

"Or 'she,'" I said. "The air *she* breathes."

"Quite," said Caspian, with a curl of his lips. "The masculine pronoun, however, has been correct for two hundred years." He paused. "Until now, of course."

"Yeah," said Carter. "That means you're a FREAK, Henrie. You might have a boy's name, but you don't belong here. Not now, not ever. This is a House of Boy Heroes. No one wants you here. You know that, don't you?"

"And what makes you such a hero, Carter?" I said. "Or you, Finn?"

"What would you know?" said Carter. "You're named after a thief."

"Yeah, a thieving thief," said Finn.

"Boys, Henrie," said Caspian, standing between us. "I know this is difficult. For us all. But family is paramount. It overcomes everything. As it always has. We must be patient with Henrie. She has much to learn."

"But where's Alex?" I said, looking around me. "I need to tell him something. Something really important."

Octavia Melchior's words were still thumping about in my head. His words about my parents and what he had done to them – to me – needed to settle deep inside me before I could bring them back up and see what I really thought of them. But the words about Alex Fischer's dad were different. I could do something about these. Something right now.

"Who's Alex?" said Finn.

"Alex Fischer," I said. "He came here with me."

"Well, he's not here now," said Finn, looking around him everywhere.

"Come out, come out, wherever you are," said Carter, pretending to look under the table and chairs.

I ignored him and turned to Finn. "We left him in a room, with maps and computers and hero stuff," I said.

"Our classroom?" said Finn. "He's not there now. I took some books back when the dinner gong went. It was empty."

Albert Abernathy was in the corner, leaning into conversation with Caspian. I walked over to them. "Where's Alex, Mr. Abernathy?"

"Who?" he said, raising his eyebrow.

"Alex Fischer," I said, loudly, starting to get annoyed. "The boy who came with me. The boy who chucked milk at you and stained your favorite jacket."

I looked at him. He was still wearing a ruby-red jacket, but the sleeves were lined with blue, not green. It was a different jacket. He must have changed it when I was with Octavia Melchior. What else had he had time to do while I was with my grandfather?

"But, Henrie," said Albert Abernathy. "You didn't arrive with a boy. You came here alone."

"WHAT?" I shouted, staring at him. "You know that's

141

not true. Why are you saying that?"

My head was thumping. What was happening?

"Calm down, Henrie," said Caspian, standing up and trying to take my arm. "Shouting won't help."

"Ask Andrews," I said, shrugging off Caspian's grip. "The driver. He picked us up from the airport. He saw Alex."

"Finn, please fetch Andrews," said Albert Abernathy.

Finn ran out of the room as fast as he could.

The seconds inched by as we waited for him to return with Andrews. I stood in the corner of the room, my brain short-circuiting. No one looked at me. It was as if *I* was being really embarrassing. As if *I* was in the wrong.

Andrews arrived from downstairs a few minutes later, buttoning up his jacket.

"Yes, Mr. Abernathy?" he said, pulling himself up straight.

"I'm sorry to interrupt your evening, Andrews," said Albert Abernathy, "but we have a small situation."

"It's not a *small* situation," I said. "It's an ENORMOUS situation."

"Did you or did you not collect passengers from the jet this afternoon?" said Albert Abernathy.

"Yes, Mr. Abernathy, sir," said Andrews. "You know I did."

"And how many passengers did you collect?" said Albert Abernathy.

"Why, two," said Andrews. "You and the young miss here." He pulled out his limo log from the inside pocket of his jacket. "Here it is in black-and-white. My instructions were to collect two passengers from a 6:00 p.m. flight."

"But you didn't know Alex would be there too," I said in a rush. "You thought you were picking up two people but when you arrived there were three. Me, Albert Abernathy and Alex. Alex bumped his head and you asked him if he was okay. Remember?"

"Why, no, miss," he said. "It was just the two of you. You and Mr. Abernathy here."

"That's a lie," I screamed, staring at all of them. "What have you done with Alex?"

The room echoed with my words.

Finn looked at his feet and Carter smirked at me. I bet you can imagine the kind of smirk he smirked. It was the kind that said, "I know something you don't. Loser!"

It told me I wasn't imagining it. They'd done something with Alex. Hidden him away. Or … maybe … something even worse.

"I want to see my grandfather," I said. "He'll believe me."

I ran to the door but Caspian stepped in front of it

143

and Carter and Finn stood behind me. I was surrounded.

"I'm afraid that's not possible, Henrie," said Caspian. "I'd suspected mental instability ran in Persephone's family, certainly after Ellie's paranoid actions at the hospital. This little display of yours seems to confirm my suspicions."

"That's not true," I shouted. "You're all telling lies. Big lies."

"I think you need something to help you relax," said Caspian. "Something to help you sleep. You're obviously tired and emotional."

He looked above my head and nodded.

I turned and felt a sharp prick in my arm at the same time.

And then ... nothing.

Chapter Fifteen

Midnight in the Garden of Melchior

THE FIRST STONE on the window woke me.

I thought it was a sound of the night – the crack of a scuttling animal in the underbrush, or the cry of a lonely owl. But then I heard another sound. And another.

Someone's throwing stones at the window, I thought.

And in the moment between this thought and the next, the memory of what had happened in the dining room came rushing back at me.

Alex. Missing. Needle. Nothing.

I looked around. I was in a large four-poster bed. Heavy velvet curtains hung across the windows but a lean line of light shone through the folds.

I climbed slowly out of bed. My head and legs were lumps of concrete.

I checked the door. I couldn't believe it. They'd locked me in.

I stumbled toward the window, pulled back the curtains and peered outside.

It was a black night. Slivers of moonlight crisscrossed the lawn and tendrils of mist wound between the branches of the trees.

Someone was standing below my window with a flashlight. I couldn't see who it was. They were too far away.

The person flicked the flashlight on and off. On and off. Short, pause. Short, short, long … The same sequence, repeated over and over. I gasped. I knew those long-short-longs. It was Morse code.

I'd won the annual Morse-code-a-thon at Girl Guides and our guide leader Goanna said I should be a spy when I grew up.

Note to you
I also won the Girl Guide Cookie Eating Competition so I could be a Cookie Taster too.
It's tough being talented.

There was a desk in the corner of the room. I opened the drawer and found a piece of paper and a pencil, perched on the windowsill and wrote down the Morse code.

Then I wrote down the corresponding letters:

M ... E .../... E ... L ... L ... I ... E

I looked down at the letters I'd written.

ME. ELLIE

We were still hugging ten minutes after Ellie had clambered up the creepers covering the outside of the mill and tumbled in through the window.

I was so very pleased to see her. And even though she was still ANGRY at me ...

Note to you

Ellie said MIND-BLOWINGLY FURIOUS was much closer to her state of mind. I reminded her that this was my story and she could write her own story if she wanted more explosive adjectives.

… I could tell she was super pleased to see me too. She kept sniffing and wiping her eyes with a tissue.

Without even breathing between my words, I filled Ellie in on everything that had happened since Alex Fischer and I met Albert Abernathy at Poole Street Station.

It felt like a lifetime ago, but it was only about seven hours. Funny how time can do that. Some minutes feel like you're falling through them in slow motion, while others huddle together so tightly you leapfrog over a whole bunch of them at once.

"How did you know I was here?" I said.

"I found the postcard from Albert Abernathy in the trash," said Ellie. "He must have written his travel details on top of it because when I rubbed a pencil over it there it was – his flight time. I went to the airfield, talked a nice pilot into showing me the flight manifesto, caught the next plane out, hired a car, and here I am."

"Clever," I said.

"I thought so," said Ellie. "But you knew I'd turn the world upside down to find you."

I leaned into her. I did.

She sighed and sat back on the bed. "I can't believe they drugged you."

"Me neither," I said. I'd never been drugged before.

"How dare they," said Ellie. "We're not going to

148

let them get away with that. It's outrageous."

"They think they can get away with anything," I said.

"I'm afraid you can't trust the Melchiors," said Ellie. "They're like a giant octopus, foraging through the kelp for frightened fish."

"Are we the fish?" I said.

"They might think so," she said. "But you and me, we don't scare easily." She smiled. "I need to fill you in on a few things, don't I?"

I nodded. I'd been waiting a long time to hear this story too.

Ellie leaned against the headboard on the bed. "Well, the drama began as soon as Persephone met Max. We suspected there was something not quite right about the Melchiors, but Persephone loved Max and love ignores warning signs, Henrie. That's just the way it is." She pushed a strand of hair away from my eyes. "But that family." She frowned. "That *brother*."

"You should hear what he says about you," I said, resting my head on her shoulder.

Ellie put her arm around me. "It was mutual mistrust at first sight. As the second son, Caspian was itching to get his hands on as much power as possible. I'm sure he'd have pushed Max under a train if he'd had the chance. When Persey found out she was pregnant, she was fearful for their baby. All that firstborn baby boy rubbish. She made me promise that if by some remote chance their baby was a girl, I would take the baby from the hospital as soon as she was born."

"But why?" I said.

"Sometimes, the threat of danger is as powerful as danger itself," said Ellie. "Persey didn't know what would happen to a baby girl in the Melchior family. She wanted to make sure you would be safe first, to get assurances from the whole family before they brought you home. She tried to talk to Max about this before you were born but he thought she was just having pre-birth wobbles. Like all of them, he was utterly convinced their baby would be a boy. As it had been for two hundred years."

Boy, was I a disappointment, I thought.

"So Persey and I devised a plan. I would take you and hide you for a few days. And when it was safe, she would send me a sign."

"What sign?" I said.

"A postcard saying WISH YOU WERE HERE, with the time and the date, and then we'd meet at Rex Pier, by the old pavilion."

"So the postcard never came?" I said.

"No, it came all right," said Ellie. "When you were

two weeks old. And off we went, you bundled up in your best clothes. We waited and waited, until your little nose was blue with cold, but Persey never came." She paused. "And now we know why."

"Octavia Melchior told them I was dead," I said.

"They must have been heartbroken," said Ellie. "They loved you very much, you see. I tried to contact them but the castle in Moldavia was vacant and nobody had ever heard of HoMe. The Melchiors are very secretive. Always writing each other notes in codes. And you and I moved a lot in those first years. I always left a forwarding address, of course. I kept believing Persey would find us. But now I understand why she didn't. Why she couldn't." Ellie took my hand. "That kind of heartbreak, Henrie," she said, "it explodes on the inside, and it takes a very long time to put yourself back together. And even then, you're never quite who you were before."

"I miss my mum and I've never even met her," I said.

"I miss her too," said Ellie. "There's something special about Persey."

"What do you mean?" I said.

"Well," said Ellie, thinking, "it's like she ... sparkles."

"Sparkles?"

"As though she's powered inside by thousands of fairy lights," said Ellie.

I smiled. I loved fairy lights.

"And when you're near her," said Ellie, "that sparkle, that joy, spreads to you."

"What else?" I said. "Tell me about my mum."

"She loves daffodils and caramel shortbread," said Ellie.

"Me too."

"She makes a mean fish pie," said Ellie.

"Yum."

"She's funny and brave, and totally fierce about those she loves." Ellie paused. "And when *you* smile, you look just like her."

Just like her.

I smiled. Extra wide. So Ellie could see my mum in me.

"I'm truly sorry, Henrie," said Ellie, holding me tight. "I wanted to tell you about all this, but it became lodged so deep inside me I sometimes forgot it was there. You and I had our life together and suddenly eleven years had passed."

"Do you think people can change?" I said.

"You mean your grandfather?" said Ellie.

I nodded.

"Maybe," said Ellie. "If he really wants to."

"I think he does," I said. "I hope he can."

"Me too," said Ellie.

We heard it at the same time. Footsteps on the stairs.

I gripped Ellie. "Someone's coming," I whispered.

She jumped up and looked around the room.

"Quick," I said. "The wardrobe."

She sprinted across the room and yanked the wardrobe

door open. With a half wave, she disappeared inside.

I listened as the footsteps came closer and closer. Then I heard a muffled scream and a crashing noise – from the wardrobe.

"Ellie? Are you okay? ELLIE!" I whispered as loudly as I could.

I started toward the wardrobe, but a key was already turning in the lock.

The door opened.

Chapter Sixteen
Things Fall Apart

IT WAS ALBERT Abernathy.

His face was pale and his shirt was hanging out.

He didn't look like himself.

"What is it?" I said, leaping off the bed. "What's happened?"

"It's your grandfather, Henrie," he said. "His heart. The ambulance has just arrived."

I ran from the room, Albert Abernathy following close behind. We hurtled down the spiral staircase into the hall, which was crowded with people.

My grandfather was in the middle of the hall, lying on a stretcher with an oxygen mask covering his face. Caspian was organizing the medics, and Carter and Finn were hovering in the background.

I rushed over to the stretcher.

My grandfather's eyes were closed and his breathing was raspy.

A wisp of hair stood up on his head. The front door was open and a cool breeze had snuck in, blowing Grandfather's wisp to the left and then to the right. I smoothed it down and put my hand on his head, trying to keep it warm.

He made a small sound and my heart somersaulted. I held his hand.

"Grandfather," I said, leaning close to him. "It's me, Henrie. Can you hear me?"

His eyes fluttered beneath his eyelids and he smiled weakly. "Henrie," he whispered.

"Yes, it's me," I said. "I'm here."

"Find ... Will," he said.

Will? I thought. *Who's Will?*

He tried to say something else but the words disappeared in his throat – as if they were too tired to leap up and out of his mouth.

I thought of all the words Grandfather and I still had to say to each other. Words I didn't even know I wanted to say yet. Words that now might never be said.

I watched his chest rise and fall. The pauses between his breaths seemed to be getting longer. As though his body was forgetting, slowly, how to breathe.

Someone tapped me on the shoulder and moved me, gently, to the side. It was the ambulance man. "We have to take him to the hospital now," he said.

I leaned over and kissed my grandfather's forehead.

"I forgive you," I whispered.

We waited in the family room, Finn, Carter, Albert Abernathy and me. Caspian had gone to the hospital in the ambulance with Grandfather.

The hours of the night passed in a blur. I kept thinking of Octavia. Lying so still on the stretcher. As though he had already gone somewhere else, far away from us.

I needed to get back to my room to find out what had happened to Ellie, but I couldn't leave now. Not while we waited for news of Grandfather. And what about Alex? Where was he? This was a house of disappearing people.

I looked at Finn and Carter. They were sprawled, half asleep, on the couch. I didn't like them and they didn't like me. But that didn't mean they would hurt Alex, did it?

Then I remembered they'd drugged me. Ellie was right. We couldn't trust them.

I must have dozed off because the next thing I knew I was alone in the room and Albert Abernathy was shaking me awake. I knew from his face what he had to say.

"I'm sorry, Henrie," he said. "Your grandfather died peacefully a few hours ago."

I stared at him as the words repeated in my head. They made me feel hollow. As if something essential, something I hadn't even known was part of me, had evaporated on the inside.

"Meeting you gave Octavia great comfort," said Albert Abernathy, patting my shoulder. His eyes were teary and his words were heavy with sadness.

"Me too," I mumbled.

He straightened himself up and looked at his watch. "It has been a long night," he said. "The boys are having breakfast. I suggest you join them. Family can be a comfort at a time like this."

He led me into the dining room where Carter and Finn were filling up on bacon and eggs and hash browns. How could they eat at a time like this?

"I'll ask Cook to bring you some tea with sugar," said Albert Abernathy, pulling out a chair for me. "I know this is a shock."

"Thank you," I said.

As soon as Albert Abernathy had left the room,

Finn turned to me with a mouth full of half-chewed hash browns. "Dad said we'll be running HoMe now."

"Shut up, Finn," said Carter. "Dad told us not to talk about it yet."

"Octavia has only just died," I said. "Haven't you got any feelings?"

"Feelings are for girls," said Carter.

Finn sniggered.

I couldn't stay near them any longer. "I'm going to my room," I said, pushing back my chair.

"Suit yourself," said Carter.

"Yeah," said Finn. "You won't be here for much longer."

I stomped out of the room and was heading up the staircase to look for Ellie when I heard raised voices. They were coming from Grandfather's study.

I tiptoed down the staircase and stood outside the door so I could listen through the keyhole. There were two voices. One, loud and angry. The other, calm and low.

It was Caspian and Albert Abernathy.

"Where is it?" shouted Caspian. I could hear drawers being opened and closed. Or maybe being thrown on the floor. He was a walking, talking tornado.

"He's changed it. I know he has," said Caspian. "She's going to ruin everything."

"You don't know that, Caspian," said Albert Abernathy.

"He had very little time with her, after all."

"As if that matters," said Caspian. "Max was always his favorite. And now Max's daughter has popped up out of nowhere to take his place. All these years I've slaved for HoMe, and what do I get? What do my boys get? Nothing!"

There was a crash.

"Calm down, Caspian," said Albert Abernathy. "You're upset."

"Of course I'm upset," screamed Caspian. "Even in death, my father is still controlling us."

I thought of my grandfather's last words to me: *Find Will.*

Maybe Will wasn't a person after all. Maybe Octavia had been talking about his will. I think he wanted me to find it.

Before Caspian.

I jumped out of the way as the door opened suddenly and Caspian burst through it.

"Henrie," he said, stopping mid-step.

"Yes," I squeaked.

"What are you doing here?" he said, standing over me.

"I'm ... um ... I'm ... looking for ... you," I said.

"Well, you've found me," he said, frowning. "What do you want?"

160

"I … I …" I stuttered.

"Ah, Henrie," said Albert Abernathy, sliding around the corner to stand beside Caspian. "Good. You've found us."

"We've established that, Abernathy," said Caspian, his voice flat and angry.

"I suggested to Henrie that she attend Hero School with the boys this morning," said Albert Abernathy. "For Finn and Carter's sake – and for you too, of course, Henrie – we should try to carry on as normally as possible. For the time being, anyway."

Caspian looked at his watch. "Is that really necessary?"

"It is," said Albert Abernathy. "Year Six Hero exams are only a few weeks away. The boys can't afford to miss lessons." He paused. "Well, Finn can't afford to anyway. I'll tell the boys it's school as usual." He turned to me. "You might find this of interest, Henrie," he said, giving me a copy of *The Hero's Handbook*.

"Very well then," said Caspian, snapping his heels in irritation as he turned and walked away. "We begin class in ten minutes, Henrie. Do not be late."

HERO SCHOOL HERE

Chapter Seventeen
Hero School

I WASN'T LATE to class. I was early.

> `The Hero's Handbook`
> `Top Tip 2: The early hero catches`
> `the clue.`

That Hero top tip got me thinking. Maybe Alex had left me a clue in the classroom? Like a chalk arrow on the floor, pointing me in the right direction?

> `The Hero's Handbook`
> `Top Tip 3: Clues can be constructed`
> `from all kinds of materials:`
> `* In the kitchen, create a trail of`
> `bread crumbs (brown bread is best),`

or write an invisible message with
lemon juice.
* In the bathroom, carve a clue in the
soap, or write a message in the steam
from the shower.

I poked my head around the door: the classroom
was empty. I scanned it from back to front, side to side,
looking for anything that was out of place. I lifted up
the lid of the first desk and rummaged around until
I touched a moldy old apple core. Gross!

I looked for footprints or blood splatters on the floor,
but the only thing out of place was a candy wrapper
lying under the desk by the window.

The Hero's Handbook
Top Tip 11: Sometimes, things are not
what they seem.

I picked it up, smoothed it out and held it up to the
window, but there was nothing written on the inside, or
the outside, of the wrapper.

The Hero's Handbook
Top Tip 12: Sometimes, things are just
what they seem.

The wrapper wasn't a clue, but it did tell me something: there was a litterbug about.

I spied a trash can at the front of the classroom and went to put the wrapper in it. I dropped it in and was about to turn away when a corner of white caught my eye. There was a piece of paper already in the trash can, scrunched up in the bottom.

The Hero's Handbook
Top Tip 18: Trash cans ooze with details. They also ooze with detritus. A hero must deduce which is which.

PS: They can smell the same.

Was it a note from Alex? Did he scrawl it in a hurry when danger overtook him? I grabbed the note and, with shaking hands, began to read it, but it was only a shopping list, and not a very interesting one at that.

The door opened and Caspian strode into the room. I threw the note back in the trash and sat down at a desk at the back of the classroom.

Caspian stared at me and, without speaking, started to write on the blackboard. Two seconds later, Carter and Finn walked into the classroom.

"What's she doing here?" said Carter, pointing at me.

"Henrie is joining us for today's class," said Caspian, continuing to write on the blackboard.

"But Dad–" said Carter.

"This is not negotiable, Carter," said Caspian. He blew the chalk off his fingers and turned to face us. We read the writing on the blackboard behind him.

Name the TWO qualities on which HoMe was founded

"Kindness and Courage," said the boys together.

"We know all this, Dad," said Finn. "When are we going to do some real hero stuff?"

"When you have finished Year Twelve," said Caspian. "Your Year Six exams are in three weeks. You are nearly halfway there." He paused and looked to his right. "Although some of you are further away than others," he said.

I thought he was talking about me, but then I realized he was looking at the Hero Leaderboard, hanging on the side of the room.

Finn blushed. I think he realized Caspian was talking

about him too. Albert Abernathy told me Finn was older than Carter by fourteen months, but it was Carter who was racing up the leaderboard.

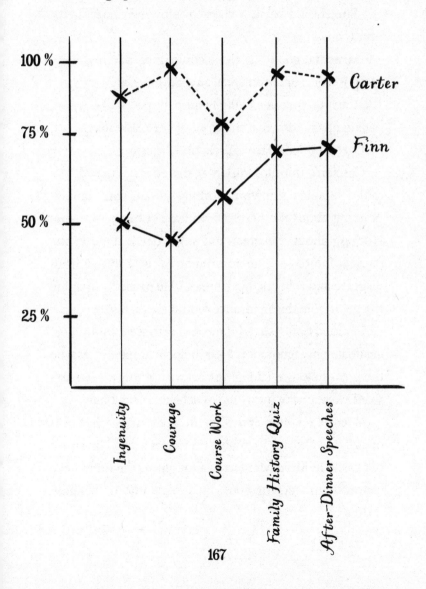

"We've been reciting Hero Theory since we could talk, Dad," said Carter.

"Henrie hasn't," said Caspian.

"She should be in a class for slow learners, then," said Finn.

Carter laughed. "Yeah. I could give her my Early Hero Reader: *Susan and Sam Save Scaredy Cat.*"

"Can you imagine being Henrie, boys?" said Caspian, pacing up and down at the front of the classroom.

Carter pulled a face. "Yuck, no," he said.

Caspian's thin lips curled at the edges. "Indeed," he said. "Imagine knowing nothing about your family? Nothing about the heroes who have come before you. Nothing about the great and small deeds done in the name of HoMe. The multitude of lives saved from disgrace and ruin and heartbreak." He paused. "Imagine the great hole this ignorance would create inside you."

Finn and Carter stared at me, trying to see the great hole created by my ignorance. I stared down at me too. Maybe the great hole was sitting just below my heart? Caspian's words were giving me a kind of ache there right now.

"Henrie's father and I sat in a classroom like this once," said Caspian, perching on Carter's desk, "in a cold old castle in Moldavia. Octavia taught us the same hero lessons I am teaching you." He looked out the window and smiled. "Max said we were Knights of the House of Melchior. We swore a blood oath – up in the castle's turret beneath a full moon – that we would carry on the traditions of HoMe. Together."

I leaned forward to catch Caspian's every word. He was talking about my dad. I wanted so much to hear about my dad.

"Max was a dreamer," he said, turning back to us, his face tight. "He was soft. No wonder he was the first Melchior in two hundred years to have a girl. But we could have coped – even with that – if Max hadn't betrayed everything we stood for."

"What do you mean?" I said, my face flaming, my voice loud. "My dad didn't betray anyone."

"When it came time to choose," said Caspian, in a low voice, "Max walked away from HoMe. He chose Persephone over us." He looked at the boys. "*Fortes fortuna iuvat,*" he said.

"Fortune favors the brave," said the boys.

Caspian thumped the desk and we all jumped. "The brave make sacrifices," he said. "We must all make sacrifices for the greater good of HoMe."

"Yes, Dad," said the boys.

There was a knock at the door, and Albert Abernathy put his head into the classroom.

"Caspian, may I have a word, please?" he said.

"Continue with your reading," said Caspian, following Albert Abernathy out of the classroom.

I slumped back in my chair. My dad sounded like the best kind of hero to me: loyal and gentle and brave, and he loved my mum. I reckoned all kinds of people could be heroes.

"Being born into a House of Heroes doesn't make you a hero," I said.

"Yes, it does," said Carter. "Well, it does for Finn and me anyway. Have you got to the quiz in Chapter Two of *The Hero's Handbook* yet?"

"Not yet," I said.

Carter grabbed my handbook and opened it at page thirty-two. He shoved it back into my hands and I read from the top of the page.

Chapter Two: The HoMe Hero Test

1) Are you a boy?

2) Is your last name Melchior?

3) Do you eat heroic deeds for breakfast?

4) Are your favorite words "sacrifice," "secrecy" and "subterfuge"?

5) What does "Fortes fortuna iuvat" mean?

Answers:
Five out of five:
Congratulations. You are a hero.
Four and below:
Commiserations. You are not a hero. You will never be a hero. Stop reading **The Hero's Handbook** now.

"But that's not fair," I said, looking up at him. "I'll never get five out of five."

Carter grinned. "That's right," he said. "You won't. You don't belong here. Just like your mother."

"Where's *your* mother then?" I said.

"She left," said Finn. "When we were–"

"Shut up, Finny," said Carter, swirling around. "We don't talk about her. Remember what Dad said. People who leave HoMe mean nothing to us."

"There's too much to remember," said Finn, sighing. "Sometimes it doesn't want to stay in my head."

The door opened and Caspian walked back into the room. "Abernathy has reminded me that it's time

171

for the weekly Hero Hunt," he said. "We've just been getting it ready."

"Excellent," said Carter.

"Yeah, excellent," said Finn, looking worried.

"As usual," said Caspian, "we have hidden a prize somewhere in the House. This week, the prize is something that may give you an advantage in the upcoming exams."

Carter sat up straighter. Finn slouched in his chair. He looked defeated already.

"You will have three questions," said Caspian. "Questions that test basic hero skills, such as reasoning, deduction and speed. The first two questions are different for each of you. But the third question is the same."

Caspian walked over to my desk. "Obviously, we do not expect you to participate in this Hunt, Henrie," he said. "You can always read a book or take a nap, if you like, while the boys test their wit and cunning?" He leaned over me as he spoke, his eyes staring deep into mine, like the evil hypnotist I saw in a movie once.

"No," I said, looking away from him. "I want to do the Hunt too."

"Very well then," said Caspian. "I hope there won't be tears when you fail. Tears have no place in the House of Heroes."

"Yeah, crybaby," whispered Carter. "Get ready to lose."

I glared at him.

"As a concession, however," said Caspian, "you may take your *Hero's Handbook* with you. That may help." He smiled at the boys. "Or it may not." He loomed over me again. "It's one thing to read about how to be a hero. It's another thing altogether to be one."

He walked up to the front of the classroom and placed three envelopes on his desk.

I stared at our names as Caspian continued to speak. "As I said, this is a speed trial as well as a skills trial. You have thirty minutes to complete three questions. The first one to complete the Hunt and come back to me here is crowned the Hunt Hero and wins the prize of the day. Do you understand?"

Finn and Carter nodded. I nodded too, although I really wanted to shake, not nod. Carter was looking at me sideways, his mouth set determinedly. Finn gave me a half smile.

"May the best hero win," said Caspian, setting his stopwatch. "Are you ready?"

"Ready," said Carter.

"In that case," said Caspian, "your time starts …

NOW."

Chapter Eighteen
Hero Hunt

FINN, CARTER AND I raced to the front of the classroom, jostling and pushing each other.

The Hero Hunt sounded like a game, but it didn't feel like one. I knew it was a test. The biggest test I had faced here. A test Caspian expected me to fail. He didn't want me here – none of them did. But I was a Melchior, like my dad and his dad before him. An accident of birth had stuck me in this House of Heroes, and I was here to stay. Whether they liked it or not.

I tore open my envelope and read the first question:

Clue 1: *I spy with my Hero Eye something beginning with LA.*

I stared at the question, reading it again and again. *LA. LA. LA.* That could be anything.

Carter and Finn had already raced out of the classroom into the main hall of HoMe so I raced out too. I'd have to think on the run.

Carter was clanking up the staircase to the second floor, and Finn was disappearing down the corridor with the Melchior portraits. I was alone in the hall. Just me and the ticking clock.

I had only arrived here yesterday with Alex and Albert Abernathy, but already it seemed so long ago now. Today, Alex was missing, Ellie had been swallowed by a wardrobe and I was on my first Hero Hunt.

The Hero's Handbook
Top Tip 24: A hero must be observant. A detail that seems incidental today could be vital tomorrow.

There had been so much to take in yesterday – all the stuff about HoMe and its heroes and Grandfather and Mum and Dad. I closed my eyes and tried to calm my thoughts, like Alex had shown me at Poole Street Station. I focused and breathed in and out, emptying my head.

Slowly, a tiny memory began to wriggle its way from the "forgot" spot in my brain. It was something to do with a name. Albert Abernathy had mentioned the name of a man who had the initials L.A.

I opened my eyes and suddenly I was staring at it. The statue in the middle of the hall. Lord Acton. The power man.

I ran over to him and saw a piece of paper nestled in his neck. **Clue 2.**

"Thanks, Lord A.," I said, unrolling it and reading it as quickly as I could:

Clue 2: Crack this code and hurry to Clue 3: JMMK PMMK

I smiled. I knew what this was. It was the Caesar cipher, I was sure, named after Julius Caesar, who wrote letters in it all the time. I bet Caspian and Dad used it too when they were kids. But how many letters along had the alphabet shifted? That was the question. I had to try to work out what Caspian might have been thinking when he set the clue.

Caesar, Cipher, Caspian, I thought. *Caesar, Cipher, Caspian. Aha! They all begin with C.*

If I started the alphabet at C, would that crack the code?

Caesar Cipher:

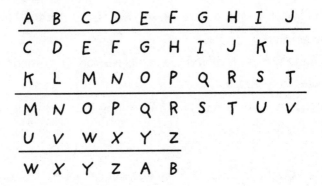

A	B	C	D	E	F	G	H	I	J
C	D	E	F	G	H	I	J	K	L
K	L	M	N	O	P	Q	R	S	T
M	N	O	P	Q	R	S	T	U	V
U	V	W	X	Y	Z				
W	X	Y	Z	A	B				

Yes! **JMMK PMMK** was code for "Loom Room," and I bet that was one of the old weaving rooms. I knew the family's rooms were on the second floor so the Loom Room had to be on the third or fourth floor.

I hurtled up the staircase as fast as I could and ran along the third-floor corridor, speed-reading all the signs on the doors as I passed, but Loom Room wasn't written on any of them.

I ran up the stairs to the fourth floor, taking two stairs at a time.

The second room on the fourth floor had a plaque outside it:

LOOM ROOM

I opened the door and walked into a large, light-filled space with wooden floors. This was probably once filled with noisy machines and mill workers, checking the yarn and the weave of the cotton. There were no machines here now; just rows and rows of chairs. It was some kind of lecture room.

I picked up a brochure sitting on one of the chairs and read it.

Huh! If my dad were here, I thought, *Caspian would be a Hero of the Second Highest Order.*

THE WORLD NEEDS HEROES.

DO YOU HAVE WHAT IT TAKES?

Hero Training 101

House of Heroes CEO

Caspian Melchior,

Hero of the Highest Order

There was information about starting dates and fees and stuff, but nothing that seemed to be a clue.

The Hero's Handbook
Top Tip 29: Clues can be obvious. Or not. Consider backs and fronts.

I turned the brochure over, and there was my clue: it was a puzzle.

Clue 3: Find two words

```
Q N V N F W Z V E L Z J S V T
K U H V D U Z G X S Z S W J Q
I R I T G E D G D S C V Q T Q
N R R C R E Y X P W M V I N B
X B Q J L K M W D T L A Z V V
J P X W A U M F R O M Q J V Z
R Y O D A Q V J H I G H E R Z
C N Q Q F O E T C L J U G I X
K W E I S F Y V Y O F M Z R L
I Z F N I L T M A B E M K Z G
B K B K U X O V W X D U G D T
H V K H V Z A D J L O Y X E S
Y W Q N G A J X L M U H R E D
N M E R F O W K B A Q R P P P
F E O V L D G K X F R L F J J
```

It was a word search with a tricky twist because it didn't tell me the words I had to find, just that I had to find two of them.

I looked at my watch. I had eighteen minutes left. *Patterns.* That's what I had to see, as though I was looking at a Magic Eye puzzle.

I squinted and began to focus on those letters till my eyes were blurry. I scanned sideways – backward and forward. I scanned up one row and down another. I scanned diagonally – backward and forward.

Ellie always said that perseverance would be rewarded, and she was right. The first word I found was HIGHER. Easy peasy.

But those letters were really holding on to the second word, huddling together to hide it. I couldn't see it at all.

I started scanning the puzzle again. Backward and forward – sideways. Up one row and down another. Backward and forward – diagonally.

I looked at my watch. Fourteen minutes to go.

My head and heart were crashing into each other and I was beginning to despair when, suddenly, I saw it, perched in the far left-hand column and going all the way up to the top of the puzzle: KNOWLEDGE.

HIGHER KNOWLEDGE. That was Clue 3.

I already knew one place that was heaped with knowledge: the library.

I raced out of the Loom Room and along the corridor. I thought I was running the way I'd come but, suddenly, I came to the end of the corridor and a locked door. It was a dead end. (I think the word search had scrambled my eyes.)

The Hero's Handbook
Top Tip 36: Be prepared to change direction.

I turned around and began to run in the opposite direction, back toward the Loom Room and, hopefully, toward the stairs to the first floor.

Halfway along, I heard voices and skidded to a halt. Finn and Carter were talking outside the Loom Room, but they hadn't seen me.

The Hero's Handbook
Top Tip 42: Shadows are a hero's best friend. Slink into one today.

I slipped into the shadow of the wall, trying to breathe as silently as I could.

Finn was pleading with Carter. "I can't fail another Hero Hunt," he said. "I'll go on Hero Probation if I do. That'd mean I couldn't take the Year Six exams and I'd have to repeat the year. Help me, Carter. Please."

"I want to, Finny," said Carter. "I really do. But I can't. Dad'll be able to tell if we cheat. He knows everything. You can work out the second question. I know you can."

Great. They were still on the second question, or at least

Finn was. I looked at my watch: eleven minutes to go.

I tore along the corridor, down the stairs to the third floor, second floor, first floor and finally back to the ground floor. I ran past the portraits of the still solemn Melchiors, and pushed opened the great oak doors of the library.

It was empty and silent and majestic. I was the first here. Or maybe I was the last and Carter had already found the prize? Funny how first and last can feel the same sometimes.

> **The Hero's Handbook**
> **Top Tip 49:** The first shall be last and the last shall be first. Deduce which end is most heroic.

As I gazed around the library, I saw the ladders with wheels in the four corners of the room. Ladders to climb higher, to reach the books on the top shelves, the books filled with knowledge. My brain screamed at me: *Higher knowledge.*

I scrambled up to the top of the ladder in the corner closest to the door – where Carter had tucked himself when Albert Abernathy and I had come in here yesterday. It was dusty up there, but the dust was undisturbed. No one had placed a prize up here. But the prize was here, somewhere.

I knew it was.

I descended quickly and climbed up the ladder in the opposite corner.

At the top, I paused. There was a narrow ledge running all the way around. To my right I spied an envelope:

HERO HUNT PRIZE.

I'd found it.

I was tucking the envelope into my jeans when the door to the library opened and Finn and Carter walked in. I pulled myself up quickly onto the ledge, like a tightrope walker, standing as still as I could, flattening myself against the wall, trying not to look down.

"Nothing to see here," said Finn, his words sounding far below. "Let's go."

I moved my foot slightly, but as I shifted I nudged a paper clip off the ledge. It flew into the air, all the way down, then tinkled onto the concrete floor below.

"Wait," said Carter, turning. "What was that?"

Oh no.

"What?" said Finn.

"I heard something."

"I didn't," said Finn. "Come on."

"No, listen," said Carter.

I froze, my whole body aching with the effort of not moving as the library filled with a suspicious silence.

"There's nothing, Carter," said Finn.

"I guess," said Carter, sounding unconvinced. I could hear him moving around the room, checking behind the bookshelves. He was below me now.

"What about up there?" he said, looking up to the ceiling. "On the ledge."

Please don't see me. Please don't see me.

"As if a girl would climb up there," said Finn. "*We* wouldn't even climb up there."

"You're right," said Carter. "Henrie's not brave enough to do that."

Ha. That's what you *think.*

"But just in case," said Carter, moving my ladder across the room, placing it out of reach, stranding me on the ledge.

"Come on, Carter," said Finn. "We've got to keep looking."

My heart was **pound, pound, pounding**, but I didn't call out for help as they left. My voice probably wouldn't have worked anyway.

I moved my head slowly to the left. I could see

the ladder. It was so close. I could do this. Well, it was more that I *had* to do this. There was no other way down.

I began to edge my way along the ledge, my steps small yet enormous. One slip of a foot and I would plummet to the ground.

Right foot. Left foot. Tiny shuffle.

Right foot. Left foot. Tiny shuffle.

I stopped, and forced myself to breathe for a few seconds. I'd been holding my breath and was starting to feel dizzy. I looked at the ladder and then at the ledge. It seemed to be getting narrower, but I was nearly there.

A few more steps, maybe three.

One.

Two.

Three.

I grasped the top of the ladder, and put my foot on the top rung. And that's when I started to shake, all over. I don't know how I got down the ladder, but somehow I did, pausing at the bottom so my knees could fill with muscle again.

That was the highest I'd ever been in my life, the most dangerous thing I'd ever done, the first time I'd felt how life and death could switch places so easily, with the careless flick of a foot.

With still shaking hands, I took the envelope out of my jeans. I was about to open it when a hand grabbed it.

"I'll take that," said Carter, stepping out from behind the bookshelf on my right.

"No, you won't," I said. "It's mine. I found it. I've won the Hunt."

"Yeah, she did, Carter," said Finn, stepping out from the bookshelf on my left. "She won it fair and square. Good for you, Henrie."

"Thanks, Finn," I said. "You too." I smiled at him. He had worked out the questions on his own after all.

"What are you talking about?" said Carter. "It's not over yet. The Hunt's still in play. It's the first one back to the classroom."

"Carter, you can't–" said Finn.

"She's not like us, Finny," said Carter, turning to him. "She doesn't belong here. She's making Dad cranky. You know we hate it when Dad's cranky."

Carter was standing very close, breathing his words on me. Finn was lurking in the background. I shoved Carter away. Hadn't he heard of personal space?

"I'm not leaving till you give me that envelope," I said, folding my arms.

"Fine," said Carter, "but it doesn't matter anyway because there's been a change of plan."

"There has?" said Finn.

"Yeah, Dad wants us to show Henrie something," said Carter.

"He does?" said Finn.

"What?" I said. "Is it something to do with Alex? Do you know where he is?"

"No, we don't," said Carter. "Do we, Finn?"

We both looked at Finn. He shook his head, but he was blushing. He didn't lie as well as Carter.

"We don't know where Alex is," said Carter, "but we might be able to find out."

"How?" I said.

"The Control Center," said Carter. "It has video surveillance for the communal spaces in the House. Maybe we can look at them to see what happened to Alex. Come on." He grabbed Finn by the arm and began to run.

"Well, why didn't you say so before?" I said, running after them.

The steps were narrow and winding as we descended into the depths of HoMe, Carter in the lead, me in the middle and Finn behind. Our footsteps filled the empty space made by silence.

"I thought I wasn't allowed into the Control Center," I said.

"You're not," said Carter. "That's why this is such a big deal. We want to prove to you that you're one of us."

We had reached the bottom of the staircase now and had turned right into a poky corridor with a low ceiling.

"What is this place?" I said.

"It's where factory workers lived in the old days," said Carter, nudging me to the left. "Kids, mostly."

"Is this the Control Center?" I said as we stopped outside a small door at the end of the corridor.

"Yeah," said Carter. "I know it doesn't look like it on the outside but that's because it's camouflaged."

I tried the door. "It's locked," I said.

"Not for long," said Carter, pulling a key out of his pocket.

"Why is it locked?" I said.

"We'll explain it all when we're inside," said Carter. "But quick. We have to hurry." He looked behind him as if he could hear something. Was that the soft fall of a stealthy footstep? Had someone followed us down here?

We paused, listening to the mill as it breathed with the sounds of the people from its past. Of the spinners and weavers who had lived and worked long days and nights, of the machines beating relentlessly.

Carter put the key in the lock and turned it.

"You go first," he said, gesturing with his hand.

Okay, I'm going to stop right there. I know what you're thinking. You're thinking I should have said, "No, after you," which would have made me (and Ellie) proud of my manners.

But I didn't.

I pushed past Carter and charged into the room. I made it so easy for him. When he closed the door and locked it behind me, I guess part of me wasn't really surprised. But the other part of me was furious.

"LET ME OUT," I cried, banging on the door as hard as I could.

"Save your breath, Henrie," Carter whispered through the keyhole. "No one can hear you scream down here."

He chuckled and walked away.

"NO," I cried. "COME BACK. DON'T LEAVE ME HERE."

Chapter Nineteen
Things Don't Look Good

THINGS DIDN'T LOOK good.

This wasn't the Control Center. This was a small dark room in the basement of HoMe, and I was locked in it.

I could tell nobody ever came down here because the air was thick and heavy, like a winter fog. Words hadn't pierced this gloom for decades. I gulped. Maybe even centuries.

It was very dark but, slowly, my eyes began to adjust and I could see the darkness had layers: dark, darker, darkest. Darkest was the far corner of the room. There was a glimpse of light near the door and I moved as close to it as I could. Where there was light there was … light.

I banged both hands on the door again. I put my ear

to the door and listened. Nothing. I was alone.

I slumped down on the floor. This was bad. I'd thought things couldn't get any worse when Grandfather died, but this was worse than worse.

I'd come all this way to find Mum and Dad. Instead, I'd ended up losing Alex, Ellie and Grandfather. Things were speeding in the wrong direction.

But I couldn't go back. Back wasn't what it was before anymore. Before the Melchiors. Before HoMe. My heart felt slow and sad as these thoughts tried to choke me. I got up and banged the door again in frustration and as I did I felt a roughness under my hand. I leaned closer. Something was carved into the wood.

When I was little, Ellie used to draw imaginary letters on my back to help me learn the alphabet. I got really good at it. I ran my fingers lightly over the indent, tracing every groove. There were two letters.

The first one was definitely an **A**. That was easy. I traced the second letter again. Was it a **B**? Or even an **E**?

Note to you

"E" is the most used letter of the alphabet.
How many "e"s are on this page?

PS: Answer on the next page.

192

I ran my fingers over the letters again. No … maybe not an **E**. I couldn't feel the bottom bit. Maybe it was an … **F**.

AF.

I sat back against the door and thought of all the people I knew with the initials A.F.: there was Allie Fingal and Arlo Fahrenheit from school. There was Awkward Flopson, my imaginary friend when I was two. But I didn't think it was him. Or her. (Awkward never did tell me for sure.)

I slapped the side of my head. I was obviously suffering from lack of oxygen. Did you work it out before me?

AF was Alex Fischer. Alex had been here too. My heart kick-started. I jumped up and ran my hands all over the wall. Maybe Alex had left another sign for me? Or a key?

Note to you

A key would be much more helpful than his initials.

I put my hands out in front of me to feel my way around the room. My foot kicked something in the corner and I froze.

Please don't let it be a skeleton, I thought. *Or a rat.*

Answer: 109

Or a spider. Or a bat. Or a very hungry monster waiting for a tasty kid like me …

"STOP THINKING," I yelled to myself.

For a moment, the silence seemed startled. Then, I heard a tapping – from the other side of the wall. I crouched down beside it.

"Hello," I said. "Is someone there?"

Could monsters talk?

"HELLO," I shouted. I knocked three times. Someone – or something – knocked back three times.

Could monsters count? Could they knock on walls? Some of them had impossibly big hands. They were often furry too.

Was it a LET ME IN or an I'M COMING TO EAT YOU knock?

"Alex, is that you?" I shouted, hopefully. "Knock twice for YES and once for–"

I didn't get to finish the sentence because, suddenly, there was a rumble of falling rubble.

The wall collapsed.

On me.

"AAARRGGHH," screamed a voice.

"AAARRGGHH," I screamed back.

I was pretty good at scream-offs. Melly Armitage and I used to practice them at recess.

I wiped the dust and rubble out of my eyes. A gray-skinned monster was sprawled next to me, staring with scary, bright-white eyes.

"Henrie?" it said.

"Monster?" I said.

"Monster!" the monster said, shaking the dust out of its hair and wiping its face. "It's me, Ellie."

"Ellie?" I said, sitting up. "That's amazing. You don't look like you at all. It's the gray skin. It makes you look really … horrible." Then I had a terrible thought. "Do I look as bad as you?"

"Worse," said Ellie, wiping the debris off her arms. "Much worse."

I shook myself as furiously as I could and the dust swirled around me in a cloud.

"Better," said Ellie.

I nodded. "Are you okay?" I said. "How did you get down here? There was a scream and a crash in the wardrobe."

"I tried to get as far back into the wardrobe as I could," said Ellie, "but instead of finding Narnia, I fell through the back of the wardrobe and plummeted headfirst down some kind of chute."

"A chute?" I said.

"Probably used for cotton bales once," said Ellie. "Your room must have been a weaving shed. Some cheapskate renovator probably shoved a wardrobe in front of the chute."

She stood up and brushed the dust off her jeans. "The chute chucked me out down here." She looked around. "Wherever here is."

"The old mill quarters," I said. "Ellie, Octavia's dead. He had a heart attack. The footsteps on the stairs were Albert Abernathy coming to tell me."

"Oh, Henrie," said Ellie, reaching across to hug me.

"I know Octavia did some horrible things," I said, "but I still feel sad."

"Well, that's because, whatever he did, he's still your grandfather," said Ellie. She turned suddenly and sniffed. "What *is* that smell?"

"Something old?" I said. "The past can be smelly."

"No, it's something else," said Ellie.

We both sniffed again.

"SMOKE," said Ellie and I at the same time. We leaped up.

"It's coming under the door," I said, pointing. "There must be a fire right outside."

"Then we can't get out that way," said Ellie, looking around frantically.

"You kicked down one wall, so maybe we can kick down another," I said, banging the opposite wall.

"Let's do it," said Ellie.

We swung our legs wide and hard, kicking as hard as we could, while smoke seeped steadily into the room. Invading our lungs. Stinging our eyes.

After more furious kicks and grunts from both of us, the wall started to crumble.

"This should do it," I shouted, with one last great kick. I pushed out some of the remaining bricks. There was now a hole big enough for us to crawl through. We scrambled through as fast as we could, emerging into a large room filled with abandoned machinery and wooden beams.

I helped Ellie to her feet. "What is this place?" I said.

"The old boiler room I'd say," said Ellie. "Judging by that." She pointed to a huge concrete thing, the shape of a submarine, beached in the center of the room.

I touched the top of it and shivered. It was very cold for a boiler. There was a plaque on the side and I crouched down to read it:

LANCASHIRE BOILER 1802

As I peered beyond the boiler, I saw a blanket folded up in the corner of the room, with a mug next to it.

"Ellie," I said. "Over here."

I walked across to the blanket and felt the mug. It was still warm.

"Someone's been sleeping here," I said. "But who?"

We both turned as we heard footsteps behind us.

"Me," said a voice.

Chapter Twenty
Like Father Like Son

I KNEW IMMEDIATELY who it was.

Timothy Fischer was tall and skinny. Like a beanpole with a head and glasses. And standing next to him was Alex Fischer.

His smile was wonky. It was an "I'm not sure if you're happy to see me but here I am anyway" kind of smile.

"Henrie," said Alex. "This is my dad."

"Hello, Henrie," said Timothy Fischer, smiling down at me. "It's so good to meet you. Alex has told me all about you."

"Well, that's good," I said, glaring at Alex, "because Alex has told me exactly nothing about you."

"Hi, everyone," said Ellie, interrupting. "I'm Ellie."

"Great to meet you too, Ellie," said Timothy Fischer, shaking her hand.

Alex blushed. "I know you're really mad at me, Henrie. And if I were you I'd be mad at me too, but it's just my dad and me and when he went missing last week, I didn't know what to do."

"Missing?" I said.

"He didn't come home last Tuesday," said Alex. "I knew he was meeting someone from your family so I hung around outside your place hoping that something or someone would turn up. Then you opened the door and asked me to come to the station with you."

"Why didn't you tell me?" I said.

"I didn't know how much you knew and I guess I didn't know where to start," said Alex.

"We moved into your street to be close to you and Ellie, Henrie," said Timothy Fischer. "In case Max and Persephone tried to contact you."

"Because my grandfather hired you to find them," I said.

"Exactly," said Timothy Fischer. "But Caspian found out and sent me a note, pretending to be Octavia. He knocked me out and stole my files."

"But why?" I said.

"He doesn't want me to find your parents, Henrie. As the second son, Caspian stands to gain nothing. But if Max is out of the way, he would inherit everything."

"That snake," said Ellie.

"I followed Caspian to HoMe and have been hiding out ever since," said Timothy Fischer.

"Why down here?" said Ellie, looking around.

"This old mill is like an amplified organ," said Timothy Fischer, tapping the pipes on the wall. "Pipes like these run through every room in the factory and whispered conversations echo through them. I've been gathering information."

"Dad heard Finn and Carter talking in the kitchen," said Alex. "About the sleeping tablet they were putting into my tea."

"Not that Alex needed my help," said Timothy Fischer, ruffling his son's hair. "He's a chip off the old block. When those two appeared in the schoolroom with tea and cookies, he'd already smelled a rat."

"Two rats," I said.

"I poured the tea into the plant pot when they weren't looking and pretended to pass out," said Alex.

"They dragged him down here and locked him in a room – one of the factory worker's quarters," said Timothy Fischer.

"**AF**," I said.

"You found it," said Alex, grinning. "Told you she

would, Dad. Henrie's a chip off the old block too."

"I rescued Alex as soon as they'd gone," said Timothy Fischer. "Caspian might have tricked me once, but his sons weren't going to make that twice. My membership in the Super Sleuth Association would be revoked pretty quickly if that were the case."

Note to you
I think I'll join the Super Sleuth Association
when I become a spy.

"Octavia's dead," I said.

"I know," said Timothy Fischer. "I'm sorry, Henrie."

"Yeah, sorry," said Alex.

"At heart, I think he was a good man," said Timothy Fischer. "A good man who made some bad decisions. And then tried to make them right."

"We'll have to fill in the details later," said Ellie, looking anxious. "The fire has found us." She pointed at the boiler room door. Smoke was creeping underneath it and black plumes were swirling into the room.

"I've got the blueprints for the old mill," said Timothy Fischer, gathering up some large papers. "There are some interesting bits to it. Come on. This way."

We ran through the boiler room, out into the

corridor and left until we came to a small door in the wall. If you hadn't known it was there you'd have missed it completely.

"Through here," said Timothy Fischer, pulling the door open and pushing us through it.

We emerged into a tunnel that stretched both left and right. A bulb above the doorway flickered on and off, and light hovered in the air. Moths danced in and around it.

"Which way, Dad?" said Alex, as we all looked left, then right.

Timothy Fischer studied the blueprints, then scratched his head. "I'm not sure," he said. "Some of the detail has faded."

"I'll check this way," said Alex, heading off to the right.

"Don't go too far," said Timothy Fischer as Alex disappeared around the corner.

"What is this place?" I said, staring into the darkness on both sides.

"It's a World War II air-raid shelter," said Timothy Fischer.

"So it leads to the outside?" I said. "To safety?"

"Well," said Timothy Fischer, frowning. "It would have once, but these old tunnels haven't been used for decades." He banged on the walls. "Limestone," he said. "Not the most stable of building materials. The tunnel might have collapsed. It might be blocked halfway along."

"DAD," shouted Alex, skidding back around the corner. "The fire. It's coming up the tunnel."

The door behind us suddenly blew in and we huddled together against the fury of the blast. A **whoosh** of flames and choking black smoke hurtled toward us.

I grabbed Ellie. I could feel the heat on my face and skin. Sizzling. Burning. Greedy.

The right half of the tunnel was now blocked by fire. We couldn't go that way. There was only one way to run.

"HURRY," I yelled to Ellie, dragging her with me, following the curve of the tunnel, left and along. Alex and his dad began to run behind us.

The tunnel up ahead was even darker, pierced by the smallest slivers of light. As the smoke burned our lungs, we gasped for air. I took off my sweater and gave it to Ellie. "Cover your mouth and nose with this," I said. "I'll use my hankie."

Ellie nodded.

We struggled blindly through the smoke – arms out, stumbling, mouths covered. I couldn't see Alex and his dad anymore. The smoke was blanketing everything. I could hardly even see Ellie, though I could still feel her hand in mine.

The roar of the fire was all around us. We were

trapped in a tunnel of sound and heat.

We ran for a few minutes more before we crashed into something. Something hard. Ellie first and me second, slamming into her. Like being squashed together in a panini press. We hit the ground in a heap.

Winded, I pulled myself up and put my hands out. There was some kind of wall in front of us. It was a dead end.

"Ellie?" I said, sinking back down. "Are you okay?"

"My head," she said, her voice woozy.

I touched the side of her face, and she flinched.

"Sorry," I said. Then I looked at my hands. They were covered in blood. Ellie's blood. She groaned again.

I looked back the way we had come, but I couldn't see Alex and his dad through the thick smoke, fringed with flames.

I clawed at the earth in front of me, digging as furiously as I could. The earth was soft, but there was too much of it.

It's funny how you still try things even when you know they're impossible. Mrs. Petrie said it's our survival instinct. It kicks in when we're in trouble and we don't think. We just *do*.

As I cast my eyes around frantically, I thought I saw a flicker of light. There. To the left of the wall in front of me. Even as I stared at the spot, it vanished, consumed by smoke. But I'd seen it. I knew I had.

Ellie was still slumped at my feet. Her face was covered in ash and blood. She was heaving for breath and coughing.

I bent down to her. "It's all right," I said. "We're going to get out of here."

She moaned.

We can't die. Not here. Not now. I won't let us.

The wall was blisteringly hot so I wrapped my shirt around my hands and ran my hands all over the wall near where I'd seen the twinkle of light.

About halfway up, I found something. An indent. With a handle in the middle. Something I could grip.

"A door!" I yelled. "I think I've found a door, Ellie."

I pulled the handle hard but it didn't budge.

I tried again. And again.

"HELP," I shouted, banging on the door. "WE'RE TRAPPED."

Then another pair of hands thumped against the door with me. It was Alex.

"What is it?" he said.

"A door, I think," I said. "There's a handle. Help me pull it."

Alex gripped the handle and we both tugged as hard

as we could, until it felt like the veins in my neck were about to pop.

Nothing happened for a long moment, but slowly I began to feel a tipping of tension. The door was starting to give.

"Harder," I yelled.

We put all the strength we had plus a whole heap more into our pull. The door began to inch open.

We kept pulling and pulling until there was enough space to get through. Fresh air rushed at me and I gulped it greedily.

The door had opened at the bottom of a long staircase. At the top of the stairs I could see another door, and bright light was streaming beneath it. The way out.

The fresh air gave me a burst of energy, just enough to help Ellie. Alex and I grabbed her under the arms and dragged her through the doorway. She opened her eyes briefly then closed them again.

Alex pushed past me, shouting something, and ran back down the tunnel. He must have gone back for his dad. I waited, holding Ellie, as the air grew even thicker with smoke and heat.

The stairwell was filling rapidly with smoke from the tunnel. I wanted to close the door, but I couldn't. Not without Alex and his dad.

"ALEX," I screamed. "ALEX!"

"We're here," he shouted, stumbling through the blaze with his dad. "It's okay. We're okay."

I helped Alex and his dad through the door and we shut it as quickly as we could. Just in time. The fire was already snapping at its edges.

"Good work, Henrie," said Alex's dad. His face was gray and the whites of his eyes beacon bright.

There was a brief moment of stillness as the four of us huddled together on the bottom step, breathing deeply. Then, we started to climb the stairs, Alex and his dad helping Ellie between them.

"Henrie," murmured Ellie, halfway up.

"I'm here, Ellie," I said. "We're all here."

We reached the top of the stairs and Timothy Fischer put his shoulder against the door, grunting with the effort. With a long, slow creak, it opened.

Chapter Twenty-One
Where There's a Will There's a Way

I **DON'T KNOW** who was more surprised.

Us or them.

Probably them because they looked the same as usual, but we looked like people who'd just been in an unfamiliar, very dangerous situation.

Alex's hair was burned and crispy and he looked like a chimney sweep. Ellie was covered in black smoke and her shirt was torn. She was still coughing up her guts and blood ran from her hair to her chin. Alex's dad had a gash on the side of his leg. I could see raw red flesh on his arm as well.

Note to you
I don't know what I looked like.

I'm hoping Ellie will describe me in her story.

Timothy Fischer led Ellie to a chair and inspected her head.

"There's a lot of blood, but I don't think the wound is too deep," he said.

Ellie put her hand on me to make sure I was okay too.

We were in my grandfather's study. His whole bookshelf was a door to the secret tunnel. Except it didn't look like his study anymore.

Chairs were upended, drawers were piled high and papers carpeted the floor. The place was being ransacked and right in the middle of the ransacking were Caspian, Carter and Finn – staring at us in shock.

"Ellie," said Caspian, with his mouth wide open.

"Caspian," said Ellie, quietly, as Timothy Fischer ripped off part of the curtain and began to wipe the blood off her face.

"Why am I not surprised you're here?" said Caspian, replacing shock with his usual sneer. "Meddling as usual."

"Lovely to see you too," said Ellie, coughing as she spoke each word.

"Someone here started a fire," I said, looking at each of them in turn.

"Is everyone all right?" said Albert Abernathy, barging into the room with a fire extinguisher. "There's been a fire in the basement."

"Yes, we know," said Timothy Fischer. "We were caught in it."

"We've managed to put it out," said Albert Abernathy, taking in our appearance and looking grim. "Thankfully, it was only in the old mill quarters and the boiler room."

"Yeah, funny, that," I said, glaring at Carter and Finn.

"This is an old mill," said Caspian. "Fires are a common occurrence."

"What about the gas can I found?" I said. "I'm sure there'll be some fingerprints on that."

Carter elbowed Finn. "You idiot!" he said. "I told you to wipe it clean."

"Ow," said Finn. "I did–"

"You're both idiots," said Caspian. "She's bluffing."

"Am I?" I said.

Note to you
I am. I'm the Bluff-Meister.

"We'll leave that to the police to decide," said Ellie.

"Police?" said Caspian. "There's no need to involve them. You've obviously had a horrific experience, but now you're all safe."

"No thanks to you," said Timothy Fischer, standing up and eyeballing Caspian.

"What's going on?" I said, surveying the chaos. "What are you doing?"

"I believe they are looking for Octavia's will," said Albert Abernathy.

"Actually, we're not," said Caspian. "I have the valid will here." He flourished an official-looking document in front of us, and smiled.

Carter smiled too.

"And," said Caspian, "you'll find it says I am the sole heir. In the event of my death, the entire estate passes to Carter and Finn."

I cleared my throat. "Actually, no," I said. "I don't think that's right. I think Octavia made another will."

Everyone stared at me. Some of them had shock jaw.

"That is an absurd proposition," said Caspian. "We've searched the entire room. There is no other will."

Heart thumping, I walked over to the bookshelf, pulled out *The Adventures of Peregrine Pickle* and opened it.

On top of the invoice from Timothy Fischer, there was a new folded document:

The last will and testament of
Octavia Maximillian Melchior

I clutched it to my chest.

It was just where I had thought it would be.

Everyone was silent as I opened it. I hadn't read a will before so I wasn't really sure what I was looking for. There were lots of long words running into each other that didn't make much sense.

This is the last will of
Octavia Maximillian Melchior

Blah blah blah.

By this will, I revoke all previous wills and
testamentary acts and dispositions.

Blah blah blah.

But then, I did see something familiar. My name.

I bequeath my entire estate to my
granddaughter, Henrietta Madeline
Melchior, and the surviving descendants
of Henry Horatio Melchior.

I looked up from the words at all the surprised faces before me. I must have looked as surprised as them.

Caspian made a strangled sound and slumped into a chair. Carter and Finn stood behind him, talking at once.

"This is preposterous," shouted Caspian. "The delusional ravings of an old man on his deathbed.

A final flourish of sentiment. Brought on by … her!" He pointed at me. "That document will not stand up in court."

All the shouting started again.

"I wouldn't be quite so sure of that," said Albert Abernathy, his voice rising above all the others. "I assure you, this will is legal."

"Give it to me," said Caspian, standing up and snatching it from my hands. He scanned the pages and then snarled. "Of course," he said. "And there's your signature, Abernathy. Devious to the end."

"If you look closely," said Albert Abernathy, "you'll see also that it's signed by F.C. Gerrard, solicitor. There's no doubt that this is an official document and the last will of Octavia Melchior."

Everyone started talking at the same time again.

"Wait," I yelled above the noise. "Wait! You've all forgotten something."

Everyone turned to me.

"It's not just me," I said. "Octavia has also left it to the living descendants of Henry Horatio Melchior. But who are they?"

Everyone was silent.

Then Timothy Fischer stood up.

"We are," he said. "Alex and me."

Chapter Twenty-Two
Past and Present

WELL, THAT WAS a stinky sock in the face, *whacking* us all awake.

It's good to have one of those in the last pages of a story.

Could it be true? Timothy and Alex Fischer were Melchiors – well, *kind of* Melchiors, anyway.

"It was no accident Octavia hired me," said Timothy Fischer. "He'd employed a genealogist to piece together the missing parts of the family tree, and that led him to me. He told me the story of Henry Horatio Melchior. How the brothers had treated him so badly."

Octavia had known all along, I thought. *He'd known about Alex. And his dad. He'd shown me* Peregrine Pickle *because he wanted me to know his secret hiding place.*

"Why should we believe anything you say?" said Caspian.

"Because I've got the genealogical proof, of course," said Timothy Fischer. He looked at Caspian. "Safe in a bank deposit box that can be accessed only by me."

I looked at Alex. "So we're cousins?" I said.

"Yeah, sort of," he said.

I smiled and he smiled back.

A slow clapping filled the room. "Oh, how very touching," said Caspian. "How my father would have enjoyed this scene. Turning the tables on me, on all of us, even in death."

"It's over, Caspian," said Ellie.

"It's never over, Ellie," said Caspian, in a low slow voice. "HoMe is mine."

"You're lucky we're not pressing charges for drugging minors and attempted murder," said Ellie. "We know you, or your sons, started the fire. We'll have to explain the fire to the police, of course, but we won't implicate you if you're gone by the morning. All of you."

Caspian scowled at her. "This is not the end," he said. "You have no idea who you are dealing with."

"Actually, I think you'll find it *is* the end," said Albert Abernathy, taking out his notebook. "I can prove you've been cooking the Melchior books for years. Skimming off money to fund a house in Greece, an apartment in Madrid, a villa in France. I think you'll find your little

216

nest egg in the Cayman Islands has been completely frozen as of ..." he looked at his watch, "... ten minutes ago."

"**YOU TRAITOR!**" screamed Caspian, lunging toward Albert Abernathy. Timothy Fischer stepped in front of Caspian, holding him back.

"This is not what my father wanted," Caspian spat.

"On the contrary," said Albert Abernathy, "I think it is very much what he wanted. He wanted his family to be the way it once was. To be great. To be noble. He didn't want it divided by petty jealousies that pitted brother against brother. Cousin against cousin. It pained him to recognize that he'd behaved as badly as his ancestors – the brothers who'd banished Henry Melchior from the family. And, sometimes, before things can change, they must end. This is your end, Caspian."

Albert Abernathy walked over to the door and opened it.

Everyone in the room was still, watching Caspian as fury filled his whole body.

"Boys," he said finally, his voice controlled and steely.

Carter pushed past me, knocking into me as he did.

"I'm sorry, Henrie," whispered Finn as he followed. "We only meant to scare you, not–"

"Finn," said Caspian, his voice cutting across the room like a whip.

Finn hurried to join his father and brother.

As Caspian reached the door, he turned and looked at me, his eyes furious and unforgiving. I stood up straight and stared right back at him. Willing him to leave. Willing him to be out of our lives.

Caspian took one last long look, and slammed the door behind him.

Chapter Twenty-Three
One Door Closes

"THE AIR HERE smells fresher already," said Ellie as we finished tea and toast in Octavia's study. "Well, apart from the lingering smell of smoke, that is."

It was the next morning and I had slept for sixteen hours. Ellie had spoken to the police while I'd been asleep and convinced them that the fire had been an accident.

"Albert Abernathy has gone too," I said. "Cook said he left at dawn."

"Well, I'm not surprised," said Ellie. "He's a wily one."

"What will Caspian and the boys do now?" I said.

"Probably reinvent themselves in another part of the world," said Ellie. "Maybe start another company. The desire for domination runs deep in Caspian's veins."

"And my grandfather?" I said.

"He obviously wanted to make peace with you," said Ellie. "And he did. I'm sure he died a happier man because of that." She sighed. "But I'm sad for Max – that he didn't have the same chance. In the end, I think Octavia genuinely wanted his family to heal."

"I guess," I said. Even after everything he had done, to me, to my parents, I had liked Octavia Melchior. Even though he wasn't here, I could still sense him in this room. His fingerprints were on every surface. The books in his library. The half-finished crossword on the table by his chair. Maybe all the words he had ever spoken here had dissolved into the feeling behind them: happy, sad, angry, calm. Maybe only feelings linger when words have gone.

"I think I'll take *Peregrine Pickle* with me," I said. "To remind me of Grandfather."

"Good idea," said Ellie.

I pulled it off the shelf and opened it, one last time. There was a new note inside, sitting on top of Timothy Fischer's invoice.

I pulled it out to show Ellie. "It's from Albert Abernathy," I said, looking at the name at the bottom.

"That old scoundrel," said Ellie. "What does he say?"

I read the note aloud.

Please know I speak from the heart. Henrie, you are home. I hope you find your parents. No one hopes this more than me. Even after everything that has happened. Actually, despite everything that has happened. Sadly, I must now bid you adieu. But before you leave, look closely. Under and over, above and beyond. Things are seldom as they seem. The end heralds the beginning. Only you, Henrie, can determine what happens next. Never forget who you are.

Albert Abernathy

"What do you think he means?" I said.

"No idea," said Ellie. "As usual, his words are cloaked in obscurity. Honestly, that man couldn't speak plain English if his life depended on it. And as for speaking from the heart!" She snorted. "I'd demand medical proof he had a heart before believing that."

"Is he good or bad?" I said, folding the note and putting it in my pocket.

"Maybe he's a bit of both," said Ellie. "I'd call him an opportunist. My guess is he knew HoMe was on the brink of collapsing. And opportunists are always planning a few moves ahead. He'll pop up somewhere again. I guarantee it."

Alex and his dad left that day on a midday flight.

They were going home. Back to where it all began, with the postcard through our mail slot.

I couldn't wait to get home either. I belonged there. I didn't belong here – where lost years pulled at me.

Ellie and I were catching a later flight so we could close up the mill until we decided what to do with it. Then, we had to visit F.C. Gerrard, HoMe's lawyer, in town. She had an address for the last known whereabouts of my mum and dad. It was nearly eleven years old, but we had to start looking somewhere. I didn't care how long it took. Ellie and I were going to turn the world upside down and inside out to find them. Just like Ellie had done for me.

We'd only just started – Ellie and me. And maybe even Alex and his dad too. They were part of our story now.

I was collecting *The House of Melchior: A History* from

the library (I still had a lot of reading to do) when I spied a paperback lying on the floor under the bookshelf. As if someone had been in a hurry and hadn't pushed it back properly into the **M** shelf.

I picked it up and looked at the title: *Making Secret Messages Secret*. There was a bookmark in the chapter on acrostic messages. We'd done acrostic poems at school last term so I knew about acrostic stuff.

Suddenly, two thoughts and one question crashed into my head.

Thought 1

Ellie said the Melchiors were always writing each other notes in secret codes.

Thought 2

Albert Abernathy's note to me kind of made sense and didn't make sense at the same time.

Question 1

What if Albert Abernathy's note was a note within a note?

I took his note out of my pocket and stared at it with my acrostic eyes.

Note to you
Can you see what I saw?

Please know I speak from the heart. Henrie, you are home. I hope you find your parents. No one hopes this more than me. Even after everything that has happened. Actually, despite everything that has happened. Sadly, I must now bid you adieu. But before you leave, look closely. Under and over, above and beyond. Things are seldom as they seem. The end heralds the beginning. Only you, Henrie, can determine what happens next. Never forget who you are.

Albert Abernathy

Your answer: _____

This is what I saw.

Please know I speak from the heart. **H**enrie, you are home. **I** hope you find your parents. **N**o one hopes this more than me. **E**ven after everything that has happened. **A**ctually, despite everything that has happened. **S**adly, I must now bid you adieu. **B**ut before you leave, look closely. **U**nder and over, above and beyond. **T**hings are seldom as they seem. **T**he end heralds the beginning. **O**nly you, Henrie, can determine what happens next. **N**ever forget who you are.

Albert Abernathy

My answer: Phineas. Button.

"Ellie, Ellie," I shouted, grabbing the note and running out of the library as fast as I could.

"Whoa, slow down," she said, meeting me in the hall.

"Where's the fire?"

She stared at my serious face. "Too soon to joke?"

I thrust the note at her.

"Look," I said.

"What am I looking at?" she said.

"Albert Abernathy's note. It didn't make sense to us because it was a note within a note," I said in a rush of words. "It's an acrostic message."

Ellie skimmed the note and my answer.

"Phineas. Button," she said. "But what does that mean?"

I grabbed her arm. "Follow me."

We ran along the corridor until we came to the portrait gallery and the picture of Phineas Melchior.

There were six large buttons on his vest, running all the way up to his neck. I peered closer. The button at the bottom was slightly larger than the rest. I ran my hand over it. It was raised.

I pushed the button. A door in the wall slid open.

"Great," said Ellie, gulping. "A small, dark space."

I gulped too. It was even darker than the dark of the room in the basement where Carter and Finn had locked me.

"Okay," said Ellie. "I'm the adult. I'll go."

"I'm coming too," I said.

"If I get stuck on the inside," she said, "I'm going

226

to need you on the outside."

I looked at Ellie and Ellie looked at me.

I knew what she was thinking.

I was thinking it too.

Everyone knew that bad luck always traveled in threes: 1) the chute, 2) the fire … This small, dark space was Ellie's No. 3.

"No, it's not," said Ellie, squeezing my hand. "My number one, Henrie, was when you disappeared. I'm all up-to-date with my bad luck. There's none waiting for me in there."

My heart lifted. She was right.

Ellie squeezed my hand again and disappeared into the small, dark space. The door slid closed behind her.

I waited, my heart and thoughts galloping.

Phineas Melchior was staring at me, so I stared back at him, absorbing everything about my great-great-great-grandfather.

He was wearing a dark-brown suit, and his shoes were black and shiny. His collar was high and starched and a double chin strained against it. An old watch hung on a chain from his vest and a handkerchief popped out of his suit pocket.

I looked at his face. It was a kind, crinkly face, as though he laughed a lot when he wasn't posing for a portrait.

I smiled at him and could almost imagine him smiling back. He reminded me of Octavia Melchior. My grandfather was the closest I'd ever come to my father.

I wondered if Max looked like Octavia, or maybe Phineas. But without a moustache, I hoped. Phineas' moustache was black and cut neatly at the edges, and he had a dimple in his right cheek. His eyes were –

I jumped back in fright.

His eyes were blinking at me.

I heard a chuckle. "Don't panic," said Ellie. "It's me."

Phineas Percy Melchior

"What?" I said.

"I'm behind the portrait," said Ellie. "In a hidden room."

More Melchior secrets, I thought.

"Come in," she said.

I pressed the button. The panel in the wall slid open again. Ellie was waiting for me on the other side. Next to a light switch.

"What do you think?" she said, gesturing to the room I had entered. "Isn't it fabulous? I love a secret bunker. So very World War II."

We were in a dimly lit room, cluttered with filing cabinets and a long table in the middle of the room. Two large lamps with overarching shades stood at either end of the table like sentries, guarding their post.

The table was littered with books, papers and two empty bags of chips. Salt and vinegar. My favorite. A pair of reading glasses was perched on a book: *A Guide to the Remotest Islands in the World*.

"This must be the Control Center," I said. "Albert Abernathy said it was top secret."

A large whiteboard was propped up against one of the wooden posts. It was covered with photos and names, dates and times, questions and lots of arrows, linking one thing to another.

"HoMe is slowly revealing its secrets to us," I said.

"Well, you *are* the new owner," said Ellie. "Or at least one of them. But I guess we did get some help from Albert Abernathy."

"Why do you think he helped us?" I said.

"Maybe he felt we needed to see the heart of HoMe," said Ellie. "Maybe he'll try to use the fact that he helped us to his advantage later. *If* we ever encounter him again."

"I'll have a carton of milk ready," I said.

"Make it cream," said Ellie, laughing.

"Let's have a quick look in case there's anything interesting," I said, rummaging through some of the drawers in the cabinets. They were full of maps of the world, newspaper clippings, notebooks and minutes from the Annual Hero Convention, held in Toronto last year.

I walked over to the small desk against the far wall. There was a red phone in the middle with a sign above it.

Hero Hotline
Heroes Only

I thought of all the calls for help – big and small – that must have come through this phone. There was a thick book on the table – a ledger of all the incoming calls.

I opened the first page and skimmed the entries.

Jasper James

Description: Roger, award-winning gnome, has been stolen. Entered into the World Gnome Championships in two weeks. Roger is unique. No other gnome will do.

Assignment grade: Bronze

Action: Spy Gnome with CCTV installed in J.J.'s garden.

Outcome: Gnome-stealing gang apprehended. Roger returned. Crowned Gnome Champion.

Olive Vanderbelt

Description: Believes she was stolen at birth and is a princess. Or at least a duchess.

Assignment grade: Silver

Action: Royal genealogist and psychiatrist consulted.

Outcome: Ongoing.

Lucy Montague

Description: Seeking her first love. No luck finding him on Facebook.

Assignment grade: Bronze

Action: Old-fashioned sleuthing methods employed.

Outcome: True love found. Wedding invite in mail.

Matt Swain

Description: Head of Neighborhood Watch
Committee in the village of Bonnybas.
Convinced neighbor is a spy.

Assignment grade: Gold

Action: Late-night surveillance undertaken.

Outcome: Neighbor is a spy. FBI informed.

The book was bursting with hope, and I knew about hope. I knew how it felt to lose someone. And even though you might find things you didn't want to find when you started looking – like Caspian, Finn and Carter – I guess even they were still a part of the picture of me. My family was a single band of color when it was just Ellie and me. Now, it was a rainbow. With storm clouds.

"Some of these cases are still ongoing," I said.

"We'd better get a wriggle on," said Ellie. "If we don't leave now we'll miss our flight."

I put the book of HoMe Help back on the table reluctantly. It was humming with stories and I wanted to read them all. HoMe had really helped people. Lots of people. Like the widow Blancmange and Lucy Montague. Even Roger the gnome. That was something to be proud of. That's why Phineas and Thaddeus had started HoMe in the first place.

"Come on, Henrie," said Ellie. She was at the door already.

I was walking toward her when the Hero Hotline began to ring. Shrill in the quiet around us.

Ellie and I looked at each other. We turned and stared at the red phone on the small desk as it kept ringing, each trill louder and more insistent:

Answer me.

Answer me.

Answer me.

Answer me.

Answer me.

Answer me.

Answer me.

"We can't answer it," I said.

"I know," said Ellie.

"Caspian and the boys have gone," I said. "There are no heroes here."

Ellie frowned at my words. I could tell she was debating something with herself. Her right eyebrow always twitched a little when she was.

Yes.

    No.

Yes.

    No.

Yes.

    No.

Yes.

    No.

Yes.

    No.

Yes.

    No.

Yes.

    No.

Yes.

No.

YES.

She took my arm and we walked over to the desk.

"You're wrong, Henrie," she said. "There is a hero here."

A thousand thoughts exploded through my head. *Who? Where?* There was no one else in the room. I looked at Ellie looking at me. And then I realized. ME? She meant **ME**. I gasped. How could that even be?

I closed my eyes and breathed in the spirit of heroes past, as though generations of Melchiors were welcoming me; Melchiors who were so different from me, but like me too.

I began to feel the glow of my family. The big hearts of Phineas Melchior and his brother Thaddeus, wanting to help people who needed them. The strength, and sadness, of Octavia Melchior in admitting he had been wrong. The passion of Caspian and my father, swearing a blood oath to the House of Heroes under the full Moldavian moon. The loyalty of my father to my mother.

But, most of all, I could feel the courage that had filled me on the ledge in the library.

I was a Melchior, and someone needed our help.

I picked up the Hero Hotline.

WHAT will Henrie DO?

Find out in